WARM UP TO LOVE

by
Elizabeth Suit

Copyright © 2024 by Elizabeth Suit

ISBN: 979-8-9897415-3-3
Print Edition

All rights reserved.

This book is a work of fiction. Any references to historical events, real people, or real locales are used fictitiously. Other names, characters, places, and incidents are the product of the author's imagination, and any resemblance to actual events or locales or persons, living or dead, is entirely coincidental.

Published by: BB Books
Editor: Alyssa Nazzaro, Hundred Proof Services
Proofreader: Jordan Truex
Cover Designer: Staci Hart, Quirky Bird Covers

To those who finally found their fairy tale ending.

Books by Elizabeth Suit

Stella's Diner
Fall Into Love
Warm Up To Love

CHAPTER ONE
Morgan

I AWAKEN AND squint my eyes open, immediately blinded by the single ray of sunlight coming through the slit in the curtain and quickly close them. After I stop seeing the lightning bolt-shaped line behind my eyelids, I try again. Looking away from the window this time, my eyes open to a dimly lit room that is not mine. I vaguely remember the night before and the copious amounts of alcohol consumed during the bar hop. I'm suddenly alerted to the fact that it was indeed a large quantity and need to escape to the bathroom. As I start to rise from the softest bed I've ever laid in, I'm instantly held in place by a very large, heavy hand cupping my left breast. *What the what?* I quickly roll my head to the right and see that I'm trapped in the clutches of one fine, Tyler Hudson.

Flashes of the night before start to invade my foggy brain. Walking into Ally's apartment and finding the recently relocated Tyler was Oliver's twin and that is was my job to look after him on our monthly bar hop. Having copious amounts of shots with the gang. Dancing on Tyler. Kissing on Tyler. Stumbling to his apartment and falling on his bed. Having the best sex of my life. Firm. Strong. Confident. Worshipping. *Wowwie.*

My body screams out the alarm bells once again and my memories drift off like the last embers of a firework floating through the air. I carefully remove his hand and slide off the bed, not so gracefully landing on my butt before hopping up and running to his ensuite bathroom. As I'm taking care of business, I notice the bathroom is spotless and there aren't many personal items on display. He just moved in and can see from the toiletry bag sitting haphazardly on the sink that he hasn't fully unpacked yet. As I'm washing my hands, I mistakenly look in the mirror. Pieces of my straight blonde hair are stuck to my forehead, my mascara and eyeliner are smeared under my tired blue eyes, and then there's the final startling discovery that I'm completely dressed in my birthday suit. Not even a streamer to protect the private parts. I quickly grab a towel and wrap it around my narrow body.

My cell phone rings from the other room. *Shit.* I don't want to wake Tyler. I haul ass to the pile of clothes beside the bed to silence it then peak over the end of the bed at Ty, who is still sleeping peacefully, before I grab my phone and my clothes and rush back into the bathroom.

My phone rings again and I quickly answer it.

"Hello?" I whisper.

"Morgan? Why are you whispering?" Ally asks.

"I'm in Tyler's bathroom."

"What?!" Ally's reaction causes me to fumble the phone, and I manage to catch it just before it hits the floor.

"Shh," I say, bringing the phone back to my ear.

"Morgan, please tell me you did not sleep with my new boyfriend's brother."

"No, uh-huh. I slept with some personal trainer guy named Grant."

"Morgan! That's not funny. It is perfectly acceptable for you to take home some rando, but my client and maybe future brother-in-law is not acceptable," she shouts back.

"Shh, you'll wake him up. I'm trying to sneak out of here."

"Am I on speakerphone?"

"No."

"Then how could I wake him up?" Ally asks in exasperation.

"I don't know. You're just very loud and I need you to stop shouting in my ear. I may have had a few too many shots last night," I continue to whisper and rub the haze out of my head.

"Did you win the turkey shot-trot again?"

"It's a strong possibility, but you'd have to ask Carlos. He was keeping score." It's then that I realize that my mouth is very dry, that I am very naked under this towel, and that I need to get out of here and somehow find a way to never see Tyler again.

"Look, can you help me get out of here?"

"No, you got yourself into that mess, you get yourself out."

"Al-ly," I whine.

"Fine."

Ally hangs up on me and I quickly dress so I can make my stealthy exit, knowing she has begrudgingly agreed to help.

I hear another cell phone ring and press my ear to the door and listen for Tyler's voice.

"What? What time is it? Now? Can you give me a minute? Fine. I'll be right there."

I hear a bunch of rustling and then footsteps coming toward the bathroom.

"Morgan? Are you in there?" Tyler softly knocks on the door, and I clap my hand over my mouth, my eyes darting for an exit plan. I have nowhere to go, so I panic and jump in the shower, quietly pulling the curtain closed.

"Morgan?" Tyler carefully opens the door and I hold

my breath as I peek out through the slit in the curtain.

"Huh," he grumbles before using the bathroom. He checks himself in the mirror as he washes his hands then walks out. I finally take a deep breath and continue to listen for him to leave. When I hear the front door close, I tiptoe to the front door, making sure I don't run into Ellen or anyone else, check the peephole to make sure the hallway is clear then slip out the door.

I bolt down the stairs and down the street to my apartment. When I'm safely inside and leaning against the back of my door, I text Ally.

Morgan: Home safe.
Ally: You owe me.
Morgan: I know. Thank you.

I walk into my bedroom and drop my coat and purse on the bed. When I strip out of my clothes, I immediately throw the neon paint-splotted tee in the trash. I never want to wear that ugly thing again. I may have to be in charge of the T-shirts for the bar hop next time. I know we went to a blacklight bar, but please, gray with neon paint thrown all over it? Not ideal for attracting men, but then again, Ty didn't seem to mind. It was probably the fact that I made it a crop top that helped in that department. And my Victoria's Secret pushup bra didn't let me down either.

As I heat up the shower, I giggle at myself in the

mirror when I notice I still have traces of neon paint in the few places Ty must have missed touching last night. I step into the stream of hot water, letting it flow over my tired muscles. Tyler was everything I thought he'd be when Ally first told me about him. I'll admit that it wouldn't be so bad to call him a boyfriend, but this complicated, emotional wreck isn't ready for that.

My heart is locked up like a chastity belt. Nothing is getting to it. Not some rando, not even a mighty fine, super sexy, Tyler Hudson. No. No. No. He is off-limits. I'm not going to do anything to jeopardize what Ally and Oliver have. If I dated Tyler and it didn't work, she'd be forced to be in the middle, and I don't need a relationship bad enough to ever put her in that position. One-night stands are for the best. No expectations. No complications.

I finish my shower and dry my hair. After I'm dressed, I gather my dirty clothes and my favorite Oliver Hudson book and schlep to the laundromat for my Sunday laundry ritual. Once the first load is in, I curl up in a corner seat and dive into the mind of the greatest criminal mastermind.

CHAPTER TWO
Tyler

I WAKE TO the ringing of my cell phone, and it takes me a minute to realize I'm in my new apartment. When it rings again, the memories of the night before come flooding back to me. I reach beside me and find the bed empty. Frowning, I grab my phone.

"Hello," my raspy voice answers.

"Tyler, can you come over to my apartment please?" Allison asks.

"What?"

"I need you to come over here."

"What time is it?"

"Nine."

"Now?"

"Yeah, your mom is here, and we want to talk about the bar hop."

"Can you give me a minute?"

"Yeah, but hurry."

"Fine. I'll be right there."

I stretch and stare at the unfamiliar ceiling above me then make my way to the bathroom. I call out for Morgan as I approach but don't hear anything. I frown at the thought of her taking off without saying goodbye. I wouldn't have been upset if she stayed. After taking care of business, I get dressed and head to Allison's apartment across the hall. As I knock on the door, I'm trying to think about what I'm going to say after hooking up with her best friend last night.

"Good morning, Grant. I mean Tyler. I'm still trying to reconcile you are one and the same," Allison stammers out in greeting.

"Good morning. How are you feeling? I'm glad you didn't get a concussion when you fell down the stairs before the bar hop."

"Much better. Just a little sore from the bruises but Oliver's been taking good care of me."

"I'm sure he has," I say as she leads me into the kitchen.

"Good morning, sleepyhead," Mom greets.

"Morning," I say, taking in the sight of Danish and coffee sitting out on the counter. My stomach grumbles, and I wish I would have made a shake before coming over.

"Danish?" Oliver asks, holding one out to me.

"I'll make a shake when I go back to my place. I would have made one before I came over if someone wasn't so impatient for me to get over here," I glare at Allison.

"Sorry, not sorry. The turkey shot-trot is my favorite hop, and I need all the details since I couldn't fully participate," she defends.

"Fine. I basically stayed by Morgan all night like you suggested, and we had a lot of fun."

"Uh, huh," Allison says, crossing her arms and squinting at me.

"What's that supposed to mean?"

"I feel like you're not giving me the full scoop."

"And I feel like you are forgetting that my mom is standing right there," I fake whisper, holding up my hand and pointing to my mom from behind it.

"Well, before you got here, she may have divulged some juicy information herself," Allison teases.

"This is too weird for me. I don't want to know," I say covering my ears with my hands.

"Tyler don't be silly. I just mentioned that I had a good time dancing with a good-looking guy," Mom swats at me to remove my hands.

What is going on here? I just moved back to town. My mom is living in my place while her basement is being renovated, and now she's picking up men in bars. I think I may have entered the twilight zone.

"Bro, you will never believe who it was," Oliver says.

"Who?"

"Daveed!" Allison screams.

"Who's that?" I ask, unsure why they think I'd know who that is.

"Naked man!" Oliver explains.

"What? That dude who tried to get with Allison! No way. Mom, how could you?" I ask.

"I didn't know who he was. He was hot and a good dancer, so I wasn't going to turn him down," Mom admits with a shrug, as if it was just like any other Saturday night.

"By the way, how are you even awake?" I ask my mom, avoiding any more conversations about her and the guy half her age.

"First off, I'm not that old. Second, I learned how to pace myself in college. Sheesh. Who's the parent here?"

"I'm glad you had fun, Mom. That's all that matters," I digress.

"Speaking of fun," Allison pipes up waggling her eyebrows. "What happened with you and Morgan?"

"Let's just say, we were definitely on the same page last night, but I'm not so sure about this morning when she snuck out."

"Oh." Allison makes an 'o' with her lips.

"What's that mean? I ask.

"Maybe you and I should have a more private conversation about that," she says, looking at Oliver and Mom.

"On that note, I'm off to the market. I believe I still owe you some cleaning supplies," Mom says to Allison. "Ty, do you need anything else for this week?" she asks, turning to me.

"You have the fridge well stocked. Can you just pick up some chicken and salmon?"

"Sure thing. Okay, kiddos, I'm off," she says to the group and walks out the door.

I turn back to Allison and Oliver.

"So, what's the scoop?" I ask Allison.

"Let's go sit in the living room." She motions to the couch and we sit.

"Morgan can be a free spirit." Allison starts. "One minute she talks about finding 'the one' and then the next she's curled up with the first guy she meets at the bar hop."

"Basically, you're telling me to not throw my hat in this ring," I confirm, leaning forward to rest my arms on my legs.

"She's my best friend, and I love her, and I would *love* for you two to get together, but I'm not sure she's ready for anything serious. Just be careful if you do decide to chase."

I'm not sure what I want to do, and I don't want to discuss anything with these two before I figure it out.

"Got it." I nod. "So, what are you two up to today?" I ask.

"I think we'll go for a walk in the park at lunch and then see where the day takes us," Oliver answers.

"That sounds nice," Allison agrees and cuddles into him.

Man, I really missed out on a good one, but I'm glad it's Oliver I lost out to. I've been working and flirting with Allison for the last five years and when I thought I'd finally get to come out here to wine and dine her, she was already in love with my twin brother.

I shouldn't be jealous. After my last breakup, I vowed to focus on the business, and once it was running smoothly, then I'd start looking for love. I've got to say that after all these breakups, hookups might not be that bad of an idea. *Nah, I'm not really that guy.*

"Have fun, you guys. I'm going to go make sure everything is ready for my new client tomorrow."

I get up and walk to the door but pause and look at Oliver.

"You're a lucky son-of-a-bitch."

"I know."

I shake my head and walk out the door. It's time for me to start my new life back on the East Coast.

❄

I WALK BACK into my apartment and really take in the surroundings. Mom and Oliver did a great job setting up the gym, but the place doesn't feel like home. I have no real place to entertain besides my bedroom and while I'm a hot-blooded guy, that's not my style. I actually like to get to know someone before bringing them home, and I don't know how I let Morgan get under my skin so quickly.

Maybe it's the fact that I wasn't sure how I'd feel about coming home, and maybe I just wanted to remain the carefree guy who didn't want to think about the memories of losing his father. I ran to California to get away from it all. I know it wasn't right to leave Mom and Oliver, but it was the only way I knew how to deal with the loss.

I sigh and decide to get my day started with a protein shake and a shower. When I return to the kitchen, Mom has two pans going on the stove.

"Hey there, Ty. I'm making the salmon and chicken for you, so you have it prepped for the week."

"Wow, thanks Mom. You didn't have to do that for me."

"I know, but I wanted to do something nice for letting me stay here."

"I think I should thank *you* for staying here because this place looks amazing. I might need sunglasses, the shine on the equipment is so bright."

"I wanted it to look as professional as possible since it was in your home."

"Thank you. It definitely does," I say, trying a bite of chicken. "Wow, that tastes amazing."

"The seasonings are in that cabinet up there so you can make it again." She points the spatula in the direction of the cabinet then continues flipping the chicken. "I wanted to let you know I'm going to pack up and go to Oliver's until my basement is finished so you can work with your clients in peace."

"Are you sure? You know how he gets."

"I do. We know how to work around each other now. We've had a few years to figure it out."

"Is that comment supposed to make me feel guilty?"

"If you feel guilty for anything, that's on you. I was merely stating that your brother and I have worked things out while you were in California. That's all. I'm not being passive-aggressive in any way."

"I'm sorry. And I'm sorry I took off. I didn't handle things very well."

"We all process grief differently." Mom pulls me in for a hug and a small portion of guilt fades away.

"Thank you for understanding," I say, stepping back.

"Let's just move forward. Shall we? I'm just happy you're back and that you seemed to be taken with Ally's friend Morgan."

"Yeah, that was different. I haven't had that much fun with someone that soon in maybe, ever."

"Do we have a love match already?" Mom puts her

hand on her hip and waves the spatula. I laugh.

"I wouldn't call it love, but she did make me forget a lot of stuff I didn't want to think about, so that was a big plus. I think I just like how carefree and happy she seemed. No serious conversations about when I wanted to get married and how many kids I wanted to have."

"Do girls do that these days?" Mom asks in disbelief.

"Some. It's almost like an interview more than a date. And it's hard not to wonder if you'll live up to the expectations. Morgan just wanted to have fun, and it was refreshing."

"You never know what could happen. Focus on settling in and then worry about the rest. I imagine you'll have opportunities to run into her with her being Ally's best friend."

"True." I take another bite of chicken and Mom swats at me.

"You're not going to have anything left for me to wrap up if you keep stealing pieces." I laugh and steal another bite.

After Mom has cleaned up and put the last of the prepped food in the fridge, she makes her way to the spare bedroom to pack up. "Oh, honey, I left a few boxes of your personal items in here for you to put where you wanted."

"Thanks. I'll go through them this week. I might not put anything up until I can get the gym out of my house."

"That might be a good idea," she says, zipping her suitcase. "All right. I'm all set." She turns and gives me a bear hug and a kiss on the cheek. "Love you, favorite first son."

"Love you too, Mom."

I follow her out the door and take her to Oliver's house. When I return, I log into my computer and start preparing for this week's clients.

CHAPTER THREE
Morgan

WHEN MY ALARM sounds, I begrudgingly roll out of bed and get ready for the new work week. Mondays are never easy, but after a bar hop, they're brutal. Carlos texted the group yesterday that I did, in fact, win the shot-trot and that I get my first round of drinks paid for at the next hop. After I got back from the laundromat yesterday, I went back to bed and stayed under the covers to hide from the hangover, the shame, and the egregious amount of texts from Ally. She's in the new relationship bliss where women want all their friends to be in the same place, but that's not going to happen. I can't settle down. I can't put my heart on the line. Not after seeing the way my mother crumbled when my father walked away.

That's why when a guy is interested, we can have a good night, then move on. They'll never see behind the façade of who I really am. Guys think I'm this hot platinum blonde with a great body. They don't know

I'm a complicated wreck who longs to find the one but won't allow her heart out of its cage.

I should be calling Ally on my way, but I'm still not ready to face her and her questions. I know she's going to want the full story as to why I needed her help getting out of Ty's apartment and then she's going to mother me, and I just don't want to hear it today. As I walk, I text Ally a fib that I have a work meeting and can't talk this morning.

When I get to my desk, I drop my bag in the bottom drawer then hang my coat in our coat closet and take a seat. I'm the executive admin at Smyth Advertising and work for Jonathan Smyth, the owner and CEO. I've been here for five years and thought I'd get my foot in the door and move up, but that hasn't happened yet. I'm currently working on a job dream board that includes something creative, being a team leader, getting better pay, and one day, my own fashion line! I'm zoning out in my daydream when Mr. Smyth pages me.

"Morgan. Alana and I would like a word with you, please come to my office," Mr. Smyth politely states over the intercom.

I haven't done anything wrong, but I feel like I'm being called into the principal's office for goofing off. When he gives me tasks, I usually just get emails or messages over the company's productivity software. I complete them. He signs off on them. We continue this process until it's time for me to clock out, and then it starts all over again each day. I rarely have to go into his office unless I'm dropping something off and even that is getting less and less with the company going paperless.

As I enter his office, the svelte man rises behind a large mahogany desk with his long legs taking him to towering heights. His piercing blue eyes keep him looking jovial instead of brooding when set against his jet-black hair. Alana, the executive creative director, is sitting next to him. Alana has dark skin and long flowing curls. She is stunning and her voluptuous body is always draped in the latest trends. She is gorgeous and secretly my idol. Their faces are set in a professional manner and not in a I'm-in-trouble kind of way so I'm hoping for the best. *It's almost the end of the year, maybe I'm getting a raise.*

"Ah, great, please have a seat," Mr. Smyth addresses me before sitting back down behind his desk. Alana smiles and I allow myself to relax into one of the two matching wood and leather chairs in front of his desk. "Morgan, Alana and I called you in here because we've had an opportunity arise that we think you'd be a good fit for. I've reviewed your resume and see that you studied fashion as well as advertising."

"Yes, that's correct." I sit up straighter and lean forward in anticipation.

"Alana came to me to let me know that she has an

opening on her creative team, and we immediately thought of you to fill the position."

"Really?" I squeak, then clear my throat and try to lower my excited voice an octave. "Really. That's kind of you to say." I clasp my hands and look back and forth between the two of them. Alana is softly nodding her head in agreement.

"You know fashion. You have great taste in clothing. You are professional and your attention to detail is impeccable," Alana continues. "Johnathan and I have been talking for some time now about how to better use your skills within the company. I just had someone on my team resign to become a stay-at-home mother and I would like to offer you the position. You would report to me, but ultimately, I'd be relying on you to set up and execute the photo shoots for our fashion-centered ad campaigns." *Holy biscuits! Someone pinch me.*

I refrain from jumping over the desk and hugging her and put on my most professional face.

"That's amazing. I am thrilled that you would think I'd be a good fit for this position and accept your offer." A huge smile forms on my face and I don't even want to hide it.

"That's what we hoped you'd say," Mr. Smyth adds. "I'll submit the necessary paperwork to HR and Alana will get with you in the next day or two to get you acquainted with her department and other staff members. I'll set up a temp for your position, so you are free to transition whenever Alana is ready for you," he explains.

I stand to shake their hands.

"Thank you both so much. I'm really looking forward to this new opportunity. Thank you for thinking of me."

"You're welcome. We've seen your fastidious work ethic and knew you'd be perfect for it," Mr. Smyth says, standing to shake my hand before ushering me to his door.

"I'll be in touch," Alana says from behind his desk as I exit.

I walk in stunned slow motion back to my desk and plop into my chair. I can't believe it; dream boards really do work.

CHAPTER FOUR
Tyler

It's the first Monday in my new place with clients and I can't wait to get started. As I'm reviewing my client's info sheet there's a knock on the door. When I open it, I'm greeted by a tall, slender blonde woman.

"Hello, are you Lauren?" I ask.

"Yes," she responds as if already breathless.

Her bio stated that she wanted to tone, but she might need to add some cardio. I make a note, then waste no time getting down to business.

"Okay, great, come on in. You can put your bag on the hook by the door and set your water bottle on the shelf next to it. Then we'll get started."

She looks slightly taken aback but does as I say.

"This is my first time working out. I've always had a good figure, but I'd like to have some definition in my arms and legs," she says, restating what was in her bio while showing off her backside.

"Yes, you indicated that on your intake form. I have

set up an initial routine to see what you can handle and then I'll adjust as we go along."

"All right, where do I start?" she asks, looking around at all the equipment.

"Get in a plank position on the blue mat," I instruct. She does as she's told, and I continue. "We're going to start at a minute and see how you do. Ready? Go."

My clients have asked me to give them time checks when they can't count the reps and now it's something I do for all of them whether they ask or not. "Okay, that's fifteen seconds." She nods. "Now, thirty." She nods but starts to shake. "Forty-five." She plops. "Okay, that's a good start. "We'll try for a full minute next time."

"That's harder than I thought," she huffs.

"They are really good for the core, and you don't realize how weak those muscles are. Now, roll over on your back." She gives me a wink and I ignore it.

"Now, you're going to lift your left leg and your right arm and bring them together, squeezing your stomach as you come up. We're going to do fifteen."

"Fifteen?" she whines.

"You can do it. Let's go. One …"

She does the fifteen and then switches sides all with a pout on her face. I'm starting to get a vibe from her that I'm not happy about and try to ignore the uneasy feeling.

"Okay, done. Now, you're going to get up on all fours—"

"Now that's what I'm talking about. Where do you want me, sexy? I thought you were really going to work me out."

"Excuse me? You signed up for a personal workout, did you not?" She looks up at me and then stands.

"Of course I did. You are supposed to work me out, personally." She saunters to me and walks her fingers up my chest. I quickly back away.

"Lauren, I am a professional trainer. I will in no way be doing anything you are suggesting. I ask that you gather your things and leave. Your money for the prepaid sessions will be refunded immediately." I gesture toward the door.

"Well, I never," she huffs and grabs her things. "I'll be telling my friends about this. You could have had a big business here, buddy." She storms out the door and slams it shut.

I walk to the door and look out the peephole to make sure she's gone, but she's still standing outside with her phone in hand.

"You will not believe this, he actually tried to get me to work out," she says to the listener and stomps off down the stairs. *Wow.*

I start to back away from the door when I see Allison's door open, and I quickly open mine.

"What's with all the slamming and stomping? Mrs. G was a much quieter neighbor," she says in greeting.

"Apparently my first client thought that I offered additional services and wasn't happy when I informed her that I, in fact, do not." I raise my brows and walk over to her door. "What's going on with you today?"

"Well, I was working when I was rudely interrupted." She crosses her arms and fake pouts. I laugh.

"Sorry. Hopefully the next person will be quieter." Allison nods and starts to close her door. "Hey, have you heard from Morgan?" I ask, and she reopens the door and leans against the frame.

"No, she's avoiding me. I'm trying to figure out why she snuck out of your apartment Saturday morning."

"Me too. I've been busy setting up, but she keeps slipping back into my mind. I know what you said about her not being ready, but she was surprisingly different. Besides, we don't need to rush into anything."

"That she is. I can't stop you from pursuing her, and I don't think I really want to. This might actually be fun to watch. Should I pop some popcorn?" Allison jokes.

"Wow, now that we're neighbors you don't hold anything back."

"Did I really before?" she asks, scrunching up her face. I laugh.

"I guess you didn't really. So, you have any tips for me?" I ask.

"Oh, no, she already got me to help her sneak out. I'm not getting into the middle of this." Allison waves her hands.

"She what?" I ask, picking up on what Allison just said.

"Uh, I gotta get back to work. Bye!" Allison steps back into her apartment and quickly shuts the door.

So, this is how it is with those two. I think it's time for a little fun. I stare at her door a beat longer as I think of a plan. My phone rings in my pocket and I pull it out to answer as I close my door.

"Hey, Ben what's up?"

"Boss, we've got a problem."

CHAPTER FIVE
Morgan

IT HAS BEEN the best week of my life. Alana has been helping me set up my office and training me for an upcoming photo shoot. I'm ecstatic.

"Now," Alana starts. "Let's go over the photo shoot and the client's expectations."

Before we can do anything else, a delivery man holding flowers walks into my office.

"Excuse me for interrupting. I have a delivery for Morgan Pierce."

"That's me," I say, rising from my chair and walking over to collect them. "Thank you."

"You're welcome. Have a nice day." He nods and strides out of my office.

"Wow, those are beautiful," Alana coos as I set the bouquet of brightly colored flowers on the corner of my desk. "Who are they from?"

"I'm not sure. I've never gotten flowers at work before." I take the card and read it.

"If you can be sneaky, so can I. – Your Future Boyfriend"

"Oh, is there someone new in your life?" Alana asks.

"Not really? I'm not sure who this is?" I nervously giggle and put the card back in the little plastic holder.

"Ooh, a secret admirer?"

"I'm not sure. Let's get back to work. I'm sorry for the interruption."

"Don't worry about it. It's always fun to have a little intrigue," Alana admits, picking up her iPad.

I pick up mine and pull up the documents Alana has shared with me.

"This shoot is for a new workout clothing line. Yet another celebrity getting in the game. She would like us to start with a gym setting. Your predecessor worked on the women's line so we're starting you with the men's line. We have several men coming in to model the clothing to see who would be a good fit as the brand ambassador."

I nod my head and look at the clothing edits.

"I'll need you to set up a mini gym area and we'll need to create poses that show off the clothing. Elliot will be your assistant."

"Oh my gosh. I get an assistant?" I gush.

"Yes. Elliot worked with Carolyn, so he's familiar with the client's expectations and should be a great asset to you," Alana explains.

"I'm almost afraid to ask this but why didn't you promote Elliot to this position?"

"Elliot is excellent with his attention to detail, but he can, how should I put this ... squirrel and get off track with his tasks. You will need to keep a running list for him to check off as he goes."

"I see. That I can do. I like to have everything planned out and organized, so I'll share my list and give him deadlines," I assure her.

"Great. This is another reason we promoted you. We knew you were reliable and always got things done even when we gave you things on short notice. And I will warn you, that may happen here. We might think we have all the shots but then need to make last-minute changes. Thankfully, most things are online now and easy to quickly upload."

"Not a problem. So, Alana, when do I get to find out who this mystery client is?"

"Oh, it's not a mystery. Did I not send you the client bio sheet? Hold on." Alana clicks her stylist around her iPad screen, and suddenly the bio loads on mine. I blink when I see the name and know I can't be reading this right. I blink again. The same name is staring back at me. Okay, one more time: blink. Nope, it hasn't changed. The name staring back at me is none other than Tanya LeBoux.

"Oh my gosh. She's my favorite actress. I knew she

was creating a new line of clothing, but I didn't know it was workout wear or that she picked us to work with," I say excitedly.

"We have worked with several celebrities in the past, but I admit I'm excited too. She's really nice but make sure you keep a professional manner with her. You can't act starstruck."

"Of course. I'll make sure I get all the screaming out of the way at home." I laugh and Alana joins me.

"Also, another warning while we're discussing this, beware of the models. We take great pride in vetting them, but some bad apples can slip through and try to get handsy. We will not tolerate it and will fire them immediately. That's also a good reason to have Elliot with you during the shoots. They tend to mind their Ps and Qs when other people are around. This also means that you can't approach them either. I know they will be attractive and hard to resist, but there is to be no funny business. We have to follow our own rules. If they have to remain professional, so do we."

"Got it. No funny business!" I confirm.

"I'm sure I don't need to worry now that I know about this secret admirer." Alana winks.

I hold up my hand to say something but put it down when I realize I have no idea how to explain something to her that I don't even understand myself.

"Let's grab Elliot and get some lunch so we can discuss the shoot."

"Should I page him?" I ask.

"Go for it." Alana grins.

I pick up my office phone and dial Elliot's extension.

"Elliot? It's Morgan. Alana and I would like you to join us for lunch to discuss our next photo shoot," I say in my most professional voice with Alana looking on.

"Oh my gosh. I'm so excited we're going to be working together. This is going to be fabulous," he excitedly rushes out. I laugh. I think a lot of things will be *fabulous* with him. He reminds me of Rex Lee from that show *Young and Hungry*.

"I'm looking forward to working with you too. Meet us in the lobby in five."

"Will do, honey." He hangs up and I laugh again.

"Oh, this is going to fun. He's one big bundle of energy, isn't he?" I ask Alana.

"He's a great guy. You two will get along well. Let's go."

Alana and I grab our purses and make our way to the lobby. Elliot meets us in a blue plaid suit jacket, dark dress pants, and a camel-colored scarf around his neck and gives us hugs and air kisses.

"Hello ladies, are we ready?"

"Yes, I have the car waiting to take us to Claridge's," Alana says.

"Ah, a perfect place to discuss our project and maybe

glimpse a celebrity or two." He winks.

Alana and I give each other an amused look. She leads us out the door, and Elliot loops his arm through mine as we follow her to the car.

❄

WE PULL UP to Claridge's, the white brick gleaming in the late autumn sun, and walk up the grand staircase to enter the dining room. Linen-covered tables with sparkling china and low-hanging chandeliers speckle the room. The host leads us to a quieter table in the back while our eyes search for celebrities. *No luck.*

When we take our seats, we are greeted by a waiter offering us a choice of waters. I ask for sparkling and some lime to add to it. Alana and Elliot do the same, and we stay quiet as we peruse the menus. The waiter returns with lime wedges on a plate and takes our order. Grilled chicken Caesar salad for me. Cobb salad for Alana. And a Caesar salad with salmon for Elliot.

"Okay, so I've brought Morgan up to speed on the client and her requirements, but now we need to go over the logistics," Alana states, focusing us on what we're here to discuss.

"So, she told you we can't hit on the sexy models, huh?" Elliot side whispers with a disappointed look.

I nod with a giggle.

"I will be on my most professional behavior and you will too, Mister." I wink.

"You say that now, but you should see the bodies they parade in front of us and tell us not to touch."

"Elliot, you're terrible." Alana bats at him.

"I know, and I love it." He claps.

We all share a good laugh and get down to business. I love how light-hearted Alana can be when we aren't in the office. I think we'll make a great team.

CHAPTER SIX

Tyler

On my call with Ben, he informed me we needed to replace the air conditioning unit, which isn't good when you own a gym in California. It wasn't cheap, but they got it installed in a timely manner. I've been working on the budget this week to make sure I stay on track here to help keep the savings deficit to a minimum.

I hit the total button on my calculator and try not to faint when my next client knocks.

"Suzanne, come on in. Drop your stuff by the door and let's get started with your plank."

Suzanne gets into position and we get started. By the time we're done with her hour session, she's sweating and crying.

"I'm sure it will all work out for you. Do you feel better now that you got all that out?" I ask, patting her on the back as she starts to leave.

"Yes. I'm sorry for falling apart on you. All my emotions suddenly came to a head."

"It's okay. Sometimes you need a good mental workout as well."

Suzanne is wiping her tears as we walk out into the hallway. Allison is at her door watching her say goodbye and proceed down the stairs. A final wail echoes up the stairwell from Suzanne and Allison's eyes go wide.

"What was that?" Allison asks, grabbing her doorframe in shock.

I hang my head and huff out a laugh as I look back up at her. "Uh, that's Suzanne, she has some things going on at home and her workout became a therapy session. She literally sweat out the stress and the tears just started flowing."

"Wow, that seems intense. Now, I definitely know I don't want you working me out."

"It's not, it's what you want it to be."

"I thought you told that lady no on Monday. I don't think she got what she wanted." She giggles.

"That's not what I mean. Some people come to get stronger. Some come to lose weight. Some come for both, and sometimes it just ends up being therapy."

"You have a gift," Allison sasses, leaning on her door frame.

"I do. Where are you coming back from?"

"I just had lunch with your mom and brother."

"Oh, nice. Is Oliver surviving my mother?"

"They're doing well. Ellen is meeting some friends and giving Oliver his quiet time this afternoon."

"Okay, good," I say, feeling relieved.

"Are you going to Oliver's reading at Barnes and Noble tomorrow?"

"What reading? How do I not know about this?"

Allison shrugs. "No idea. I thought you guys would have talked about it."

"Honestly, it's been a week. The AC went out in the gym in California, so I've been dealing with that and starting the gym here, so I haven't really been available but yes, I'll go. What time is it at?"

"Six p.m. Oliver will have seats reserved for us, so we don't have to leave too early. I'll come by about five thirty."

"Cool."

My phone rings in my pocket, and I take it out to see who's calling.

"Oh, hey, I gotta take this. I'll see ya tomorrow, yeah?"

Allison nods and waves before shutting her door. I walk into my apartment to take the call from Tanya.

"Hey Tanya, how's it going?"

"Hi Tyyyyler," she sings into the phone. "How's my favorite trainer?"

"I'm good. Getting into the swing of things over here. Trying to get used to the time change. What's new in your world?"

"Weeelll, I'm going to be in New York for a bit," she trills.

"Oh yeah, do you need to set up some sessions while you're here?" I walk to my laptop to bring up my calendar.

"That would be great. Buuutt, I also have a favor to ask you."

"I knew there was a reason you were using my real name. What is it?"

"You know how I released a line of women's workout wear?"

"Yeah?" I say more like a question, wondering where this is going.

"Well, now I'm coming out with a men's line, and I was hoping you could kinda, maybe, sorta be my brand ambassador. Do some photo shoots with me?" I can picture her twirling her finger in her hair as she says this. She always does that when she's nervous.

"You want me to be your model?" I ask.

"Why not? You're a bodybuilder and a fitness trainer. Who better to model for me? Plus, you're hot. I've only told you a million times you could have been a stand-in for The Arrow."

"He has blue eyes."

"Trust me, that's not what they're going to be looking at," she purrs but quickly gets back to business. "So, will you do it? The shoots will be in New York, so you won't have to travel, and I won't have to suffer endless hours trying to find the perfect model. I already know we'll work well together."

"I don't know. I'll have to think about it."

"I'll pay you. This isn't for free. It's a real gig." *I hate to turn down good money but I'm no model.*

"I'm not a model."

"Look, it's not that hard. You already know how to pose for competitions, so I'll tell you what to do, you stand there, you smile for the photographer, and we put out an awesome layout."

"You know I can't say no to you."

"I know. That's why I asked. So, you'll do it?"

"Of course."

"Great. We start next week. I'll send you the details."

❄

The next night, Allison and I share a cab to the bookstore and there is still a line hanging out the door when we arrive. Oliver is the real deal and I'm proud to call him my brother. I hear some murmurs and gasps as we walk right in. It's not easy being the identical twin of a famous person, but I usually get away unscathed. Allison giggles by my side as we're approached by the woman at the door.

"Hello, welcome to an evening with Oliver Hudson. Can I have your names?"

"Allison Moore and Tyler Hudson." The woman's eyes bulge.

"Oh my goodness, how did I not realize who you were? Mr. Hudson told me you'd be coming. I also have another name here, Morgan Pierce. Is she here yet?"

"No, she's coming from work and said she'd meet us here," Allison supplies.

"Okay, great. I'll make a note and make sure she gets to her seat when she gets here. Let me show you the way." She leads us to reserved seats in the front row. My mom is already there and beaming with pride as she talks to a fan. I sit next to her, and Allison sits beside me, leaving the last seat on the end for Morgan.

"Morgan's coming?"

"Oh yeah, she's a big fan. Did I not mention that?" Allison fidgets in her chair.

"No, you didn't mention that," I quip back.

Mom stops talking to the woman and gets up to hug me.

"Tyler this is Maureen. Maureen, this is my other son Tyler."

"Oh my gosh. You look just like Oliver! Are you single? I have an age-appropriate daughter I could introduce you to," Maureen gushes.

"Thank you for the compliment, but I'm already

spoken for," I reply, letting her down gently.

"Ah, what a lucky lady. It was nice to meet you both." Maureen smiles at Mom and then starts talking to a lady on the other side of her.

"And exactly who is this lucky lady?" Mom whispers. I wink and she elbows me in the side.

"You just lucked out. Looks like your tiny omission of facts just might come in handy. Especially today of all days," I whisper to Allison while rubbing my hands together.

"Tyler, what's going on?" She asks with a warning tone in her voice.

"What? I can't let that lady know I lied to her. People know who you are now that Oliver has posted you on his socials, so I can't use you. Morgan will have to be a stand-in girlfriend for an hour."

"Do you really think that's a good idea?"

"Yes, and just wait until you hear what perfect timing this is." I wink and Allison shakes her head.

"I'm texting her."

"Why? You don't want to help *me* be sneaky this time?"

Allison puts her head in her hands.

"I can't believe I let that slip. Is Morgan going to disown me when she finds out?"

"Oh, no, I'm just trying to have a little fun. Go ahead and text her so she's prepared."

Allison pulls out her phone.

Allison: *Tyler is here. Play along when you get here. We'll explain later.*
Morgan: *What are you getting me into?*
Allison: *Remember when I told you, you owed me?*
Morgan: *Crap. I'll be there in twenty.*

Morgan arrives ten minutes before Oliver is supposed to come out, so we have just enough time for our little show.

"Hey, baby. I'm so glad you got here in time," I say, standing and hugging Morgan.

"Yeah, work was crazy," she says, kissing my cheek.

I watch Maureen eye us and then turn her attention to the front as the woman who seated us calls for our attention.

Allison moves next to Mom, and I sit next to Morgan and put my arm around her shoulders. She leans in, and I'm suddenly wishing this wasn't a rouse.

CHAPTER SEVEN
Morgan

OLIVER READS A chapter from his new release, and I couldn't be more excited to get the whole book. Chills run up and down my body, and I'm not sure if it's from the reading or the fact that Tyler's arm is wrapped around my shoulders. When I left his apartment that day, my goal was to avoid seeing him at all costs, but now I'm somehow posing as his girlfriend. This story is another one I can't wait to get to the end of.

Everyone stands and claps when Oliver is finished. He is going to be signing books for the rest of the night, so Allison lets me know we're all going to a diner nearby to eat while we wait for Oliver, and then he'll meet us there when he's done.

Tyler helps me back into my coat and we walk hand-in-hand out the door, followed by Ellen and Ally. When we get to the diner, we grab a corner booth that is big enough to hold five people. I slide in next to Ally, and Ty and Ellen bookend us.

"What is everyone in the mood for?" Ally asks.

"No. No way. You can't just sit here and act like this is normal. Why exactly did you ask me to pose as Tyler's girlfriend?"

"Weeelll," Ally starts.

"There was a woman who asked Tyler if he was single so she could fix him up with her daughter," Ellen interjects, bringing me up to speed.

"Yeah, it was super awkward, and I felt it would be way less awkward to pretend you were my girlfriend," Tyler adds.

"Oh yes, way less awkward," I deadpan.

"Thanks for helping me out," Tyler says with a squeeze of my hand that is resting on the seat between us. "Did you like the flowers? I didn't realize I'd get to play the part of your boyfriend so soon." He laughs.

"Those were from you?"

"Yeah. You've been on my mind since I saw you last, and I wanted to do something nice for you."

Aw-ww, isn't that sweet? Damnit, that's hit number one to my heart shield. I've never had to test its fortitude.

"No trouble at all," I admit, trying to keep my composure while the voices in my head are screaming something about how I'm an idiot for sneaking out and how hot Tyler is. "So, I think I'll get a burger and fries. I'm starving."

"That sounds perfect. Me too," Ellen states.

"Me three. Oh, and a chocolate milkshake. What are you having Tyler?" Ally asks.

"A grilled chicken salad."

"You are way too good," Allison admits, and I'm silently replying to the voices in my head that this is one of the reasons I snuck out. I can eat whatever I want, and I don't want to feel guilty about it.

Tyler laughs at Allison. "Honestly, I'd love to have it, but my body just doesn't do well when I eat heavy foods like that, so I just choose to feed it what it needs."

"Same, and mine calls for a burger," I pipe up.

"And that's exactly what you should have. Your body knows what it needs, so you should listen to it," Tyler agrees, and I may have melted a little because now I know he's not all food judgey. Then I realize I melted a little too much and am leaning against his arm and quickly right myself.

"You don't have to do that. If you're tired, you can lean on me," he says under his breath. I nod and relax against him.

"Morgan, we didn't really get to talk the other night. What do you do?"

I sit upright in excitement to share the news.

"Well, I actually just got a promotion. I'm assisting our creative director. I'm so excited. I'll be working on fashion ads."

"What? When? How?" Ally grabs my arm in shock.

Before I can answer, a waitress approaches our table.

"Hi. I'm Lucy. What can I get you?"

We each give her our orders. She jots them down and disappears back through a set of swinging doors that I assume leads to the kitchen.

"Morgan. Tell me!" Ally shakes my shoulder.

"When I went into work Monday, Mr. Smyth called me into his office and Alana, the creative director, was there, and they offered me a position on the team. I finally get to work in fashion, which is my passion!" I cheer.

Allison wraps her arm around my shoulders and pulls me in for a hug. "I could ring your neck for not calling to tell me, but I'm so happy for you that I forgive you."

"That's terrific," Ellen adds.

"Very cool," Tyler agrees.

"Thanks, everyone. I've been so busy all week setting up my new office—" Ally squeals next to me and hugs me again.

"You got an office!"

"Yes, and between setting up my office and learning the ropes, I can barely get home and out of my work clothes before falling asleep," I explain.

"I'm so so happy for you," Ally says again.

"Thank you. Next week my assistant—

"Eee, you get an assistant!" Ally squeals again.

"Yes, next week my assistant and I will be setting up

everything that we need for my first photo shoot."

"That sounds like an amazing opportunity, Morgan. I'm always happy to see young people excel. Will you all excuse me? I'm going to run to the restroom to wash my hands before the food comes," Ellen says, sliding out of the booth.

"You know what? I'll join you," Ally says, following her around the semi-circle.

"Al-ly," I grit out, darting my eyes at her to not leave me with Tyler.

"I'll be right back." She winks and leaves me in awkward silence.

"Thank you for the flowers. They're beautiful. No one's ever sent me flowers before."

"I shouldn't have sent them when you made it clear there wouldn't be anything between us."

"When did I say that?" I ask, frowning when the memory doesn't come to mind.

"You didn't, but when you snuck out Saturday morning, I thought it was pretty obvious. When I couldn't stop thinking about you, I thought I'd have a little fun and play on the being sneaky part while trying to do something nice to see if I could change your mind."

"I will admit that was refreshingly charming." I bob my head back and forth. "But you should know that I left because I didn't want to face you. I'm not in a place where I'm ready for a serious relationship, and I didn't want to make things weird between us since we're so close to Ally and Oliver. So, I just bolted and thought I'd be able to avoid you," I admit.

"Wow, an honest answer. Thank you. I wish you would have told me that before you left."

"I should have faced it like an adult and stayed."

"Since you've now admitted that you should have stayed and that I'm refreshingly charming, could I convince you to let me take you to dinner? No strings. Just to get to know each other."

I stare into his amber eyes and see the sincerity of his words. My voices are screaming at me to say yes, but my heart is on the fence. It's flip-flopping erratically, and I don't know if it's ready for love or trying to tell me to run. *Heart, let's make a deal. Give me a chance to get to know him and then I'll let you decide what to do.*

"That would be nice. Thank you."

"Great. Let's exchange numbers and I'll text you," Ty says, holding out his phone to me. I take it and enter my name and number into his contacts then hand it back. He sends me a quick, "Hi, it's Tyler," text, and we put our phones away right as Lucy delivers the food. Ellen and Ally return just in time.

"Can I get you all anything else?" Lucy asks.

We let her know we're all set, and she leaves us to eat. We talk about Oliver's reading and how many people were there and how we can't wait for him to bring us our copies. Oliver finally arrives, and Lucy brings out a burger for him and he immediately digs in.

"Thanks for ordering for me guys. I'm starving. I couldn't leave until everyone had a chance to get their books signed." We all look to one another because no one ordered for him, but Allison just answers for us.

"We all got burgers, so we got you the same thing."

"Thanks, babe." They give each other schmoopie eyes and I try to keep my food down.

"So, did you bring us some presents?" I ask, breaking their love spell.

"Yeah, I have them here in my messenger bag. Don't worry, I know I still have to sign the others you have Morgan."

"Thank you," I cheer. "Some days it's hard to believe I'm now friends with a famous author who I've followed from the start."

"You're welcome. Thank you for supporting me. I couldn't do this without my fans. So, are you two an item now?" Oliver asks Ty while waving his hand between the two of us. "I think I saw some hugging and kissing before the reading."

Tyler and I give each other a look and then quickly start waving our hands to deny there's anything going on.

"Not exactly," Tyler starts and then tells Oliver the

rest of the story.

"And we thought our mom was bad," Oliver says with a laugh when Ty finishes.

"Hey." Ellen smacks him on the shoulder. "In all fairness, I never asked perfect strangers."

"True and we deeply appreciate it," Oliver admits.

Once he's finished eating, we pay the bill and bundle up to brave the cold on the way home.

"May I walk you home?" Tyler asks as we stand outside the diner.

"It's so cold, I was going to get a taxi. But thank you anyway."

"Okay. I'll text you about dinner."

"Okay." I lean in and he wraps me in a hug.

"Goodnight Morgan."

"Goodnight."

Tyler hails a cab and closes the door once I'm inside. I give him a little wave as we pull away from the curb. *What did I just agree to?*

CHAPTER EIGHT
Tyler

AFTER A WHIRLWIND of new clients and copious amounts of text photos of poses from Tanya trying to prepare me for the photo shoot this week, it's finally Friday, and I'm getting ready for my date with Morgan. We agreed that I'd pick her up at seven and we'd go to Martino's. Once I'm dressed and ready to go, I grab my coat and keys and head out.

When I arrive, Morgan opens the door and invites me inside. Her place is small, and the door hits the side of what looks like a TV cabinet when I walk through. I turn and face her as she closes the door.

"You look amazing," I say, taking in the short navy dress with a strip of matching material tied around her waist. Is it attached? Separate? I don't know, but I know she looks like a knockout.

"It bodes well that you met me wearing a gray T-shirt and jeans. My wardrobe is all up from there. I think my pajamas look better than that." She laughs.

"You're stunning."

"Thank you." A slight blush tints her cheeks.

"I'm ready to go, just let me get my coat." She walks past me and into what looks like her bedroom and comes out in a knee-length, cream wool coat. "All set."

"Great. I'm looking forward to dinner," I say, offering my arm to escort her out the door.

"Didn't you just go to Martino's with your mom and Ally?"

"Yes, but that was for my mom. This is for you."

"You won't be tired of it?"

"When you taste their food, you'll know why the answer to that question is a resounding, 'no way.'"

She laughs as we walk to the curb and hail a cab.

❉

THE TWINKLING LIGHTS outside the restaurant remind me of walking through the snow with my family in Central Park with the stars and streetlamps glowing in the night. We'd often take a walk after coming into the city to see a show. I ran as far away as possible to avoid the memories, and now I'm not so sure this was a good idea. I should have taken Morgan somewhere else.

"Oh, look at the pretty lights," she says with a giggle, and its melody instantly brightens my mood.

"Here, allow me," I say, stepping out of the cab and

offering my hand to help her out.

"Thank you."

We walk up the steps and I hold the door open for her, then guide her to the hostess stand. The woman leads us through the linen-clothed tables and into a booth near the back. As she sits, Morgan shrugs off her coat but keeps it around her shoulders.

"Are you warm enough?"

"I'm fine. It just takes me a minute to warm up after being outside. I really hate the cold."

"Me too. That's part of the reason I ran off to California. I think I'm going to need a thicker coat." I shake off the chill and put my coat next to me on the seat.

"I can go shopping with you and pick out some things if you'd like," Morgan offers.

"That'd be great. Thanks. I admit I have no idea where to go shopping. I was just going to order some things online." I admit, picking up a menu even though I really don't have to look at it.

"You want to try things on and get them tailored. That's really the only way to go. No one fits in their clothes perfectly, so tailoring is the only way to get a good fit. I know a bunch of men's stores that I think you'd like."

"That's not something I'd ever think about. Plus, I'm usually in sweats and workout clothes most of the time, so I've never bothered with dress clothes. But now that you bring it up, I do have trouble fitting the collar and sleeves right when I have to dress up. I admit I wear this shirt the most because it's one of the few that fit right." Morgan eyes my shirt.

"I can see that. If you tailored it, it would fit even better. Don't worry. I'll take care of you." I'm shocked by her sudden willingness to plan another date before this one has even ended.

"Thank you. I appreciate you helping me out."

"Sure thing. Happy to do it. It's my all-time favorite thing to do. If I didn't get my promotion, I was going to apply for a personal shopping job for a high-end store. I can go tomorrow if you're free," Morgan offers.

"I don't have any weekend clients, so that would work."

"Let's grab breakfast at Joe's Café and then we can walk to the shops a few blocks over and get you all squared away."

"Can we go to an outerwear store first?" I ask, and she laughs.

"Absolutely! Now, tell me what's good."

I list my top favorites on the menu.

"I've heard great things about the fettuccini alfredo with meatballs," she says with a smirk.

"You must have been talking to Oliver. I don't think he's ever gotten anything else from here."

"Well Ally, not Oliver, but she gave it rave reviews."

"Go ahead and try it then," I encourage.

"I think I kinda have to see what all the fuss is about." She closes the menu and sets her hands on her lap.

When the waiter comes, I order our meals and some wine, and decide now is as good a time as any to try to get to know Morgan better.

CHAPTER NINE
Morgan

"So, tell me about yourself," Ty starts after the waiter leaves.

"What do you want to know?"

"I want you to info dump so all the readers can get your backstory and we can move forward with more sex," Ty says with a laugh. *This man knows me too well already.* "Here is where Morgan Pierce will divulge her deepest secrets to sway Tyler Hudson to fall head over heels in love with her," he adds in his best movie-announcer voice while trying to keep a straight face and failing miserably.

"Who said I wanted you to fall in love with me?" I say, and Tyler frowns in concern.

"I—" he starts, but I interrupt him with a wink to squash his worry then move on. "Kidding." I laugh when he lets out a sigh of relief. "I don't think Oliver would agree to an info dump. I'm supposed to tell you small things about myself throughout so I can keep you hooked and on your toes. Have you not read his crime novels? I'm a huge fan," I add in jest since he knows all of that quite well.

"Did you know I've read every one of them from first drafts to finals?" he says.

"You get to see first drafts? Oh, that's exciting. Tell me more." I lean in as if I'm about to get the answer to life's biggest question.

"They're rubbish." He throws his hand up in the air for emphasis. "Absolute garbage. He'd be lost without me. I have to rearrange stuff and then tell him like it is." He crosses his arms and nods, pleased with himself.

"I don't believe you for a second, you're full of it," I say with a laugh, swatting at him.

"Good because he's amazing." He uncrosses his arms and rests them on the table. "He could publish his first draft and still be a best seller. The man's got a gift."

"I know. I heard him speak at the signing. Did you think I was too busy keeping up the girlfriend rouse to listen to my favorite author? Maybe it was you who was too preoccupied with your little rouse to pay attention," I tease.

"My mind may have wandered once or twice," he admits with an exaggerated frown and a head bobble.

I laugh. "If you don't let it go to your head, I did enjoy having your arm around me."

"My arm very much liked being around you," he

flirts back.

"I still have to get him to sign all my other books," I say, quickly changing the subject. I'm not sure how much flirting I want to encourage.

"Maybe he'll let you read the next one early." My eyes go wide, and I almost hyperventilate at the thought.

"Don't even joke about that. I would literally cry if he did. I almost canceled this date to stay home in my pajamas and read the one we just got."

"The writer trumps the jock once again," he jests.

"Well, I would say that given the fact that I'm actually here, without my nose stuck in a book, means the jock won," I toss back.

"Good point. Now, are you going to keep avoiding my question and talk about my brother all night or finally tell me something about yourself?" He smirks, leaning forward on the table.

"Fine," I concede with a huff. "You already know my name so let's see ... I'm twenty-eight years old. I work for an ad agency. I just got a promotion, and I can't wait to save up enough money to get out of my apartment." I quirk my lips to the side and take a sip of the red wine the waiter just placed in front of me.

"Was that so hard?" he asks.

"No. It's just that sometimes I feel like I have nothing to show for myself," I admit, shrugging and waving my arms around. "I thought I'd be more successful by now, working my way up the ladder and owning my own fashion conglomerate someday. All the stars would be clamoring for my designs." I laugh and take another sip of wine.

"We all have dreams, and you just made one of yours come true. You are working your way up. When I went to California, I was just a trainer in a gym when this young woman came in. She needed to prepare for a role in a spy movie. I was fortunate enough to get assigned to her. She did what I told her to do, and she got the results she needed. Suddenly word spread, and I became a trainer to the stars. Sometimes all it takes is one person to believe in you. And it sounds like this Smyth guy does. And, hey, if you want to do some sketches I can show them to my friend Tanya."

"Tanya?"

"Yeah, my actress friend. She's the one that I was just telling you about. We've been working together for five years now and she's the most down-to-earth celebrity you've ever met. Her parents didn't let it all go to her head and really helped keep her away from the wrong people."

"Are you talking about *the* Tanya LeBoux?"

"Yes, that's her."

A million thoughts swirl through my head knowing that we both are officially working for Tanya. *Do I tell him she's our client too?*

The waiter chooses that moment to bring our plates and we pause our conversation. The biggest plate of fettuccini I've ever seen, topped with meatballs, is set in front of me. The song, "On Top of Spaghetti," rings through my mind as I'm worried that the meatballs are going to roll right off the top of the pile. As I secure the meatballs with my fork, the aroma hits my nose, and my mouth waters.

"Wow." I look up at Tyler. I think he's drooling too.

"Yeah, see why this is our favorite place?" he asks, cutting into his chicken parmesan.

"I'll be eating this for days," I admit and take my first bite. The creamy, buttery goodness melts over my tongue, and I try not to moan. "Wow, just wow. I have no words to describe this. I'm speechless," I admit.

"Uh oh. How am I going to get to know you better if I've rendered you speechless? I should have thought about that before I brought you here," Tyler jokes.

"Maybe you'll have to give me a minute and then the words will flow again," I say before taking another bite.

"Back to Tanya and your designs. Let me know if you want me to talk to her for you," Ty adds.

I bobble my head back and forth in thought. I think it would be best to prove myself to her on this upcoming photo shoot first.

"Okay, let me get through this upcoming project first. It's the first shoot that I'm in charge of and I need to focus on that right now."

"When you're ready, just say the word."

"Thank you, Ty. Now I'm glad I agreed to this date!" I grin and wink.

Ty laughs finally catching on to my humor and cuts another bite.

"Me too. I'm happy to help. I feel that's why we're all here. To help and complement each other."

"Aw, you're so handsome." I tease and twirl another forkful of pasta.

"No, not like that. Complement our skills. Like Tanya can't get fit on her own and I can't act but together we make a great team."

"Oh, I see. I like that. I like that idea a lot," I agree, pointing my fork at him. "So, like the other night when you twirled me in the air and I—"

"How are your meals? Everything to your satisfaction? More wine?" The waiter interrupts.

"Yes, everything is terrific. Morgan, would you like more wine?" Ty addresses me.

"Yes, I'll have some more, thank you." The waiter nods and leaves the table.

"Exactly!" Ty says, continuing where we left off before being interrupted.

"I'll have to think about complementing your skills again." I wink.

The waiter brings more wine, and we continue to eat

around light conversation like the weather: it's too cold. And Tyler can't wait to go shopping for warmer clothes tomorrow. What our upcoming work week looks like: busy with our new jobs. And when we can go on our next official date because apparently shopping doesn't count. I agreed to go out again next weekend because I think I'm starting to like this guy.

Once we've finished our meals, Tyler pays and we hail a cab back to my apartment.

CHAPTER TEN
Tyler

AFTER DROPPING MORGAN off, I head home. Once I've changed and settled in for the night, I call Oliver.

"Hey, how did the date go?" he asks when he answers.

"It was great. It took me a minute to know when she was busting my balls, but once I got it, we laughed all night. She's taking me shopping tomorrow for warmer clothes."

"But you hate shopping."

"Dude, have you seen this girl? I will literally go anywhere she asks me to."

"You think you might have a chance with her?" he asks.

"I think so. I just need to take things slow. I don't want to spook her after what Allison said. I don't want to be one of her flings, and I need to protect myself too after everything that happened with Jordan. Which is why I agreed to go shopping. She said she wanted to be a personal shopper at one point, so I figured it was a way to get to know her better while she's doing something she's comfortable with."

"That's slick. So, I shouldn't mention it's your worst nightmare when I see her next?" Oliver laughs.

"Funny. Don't ruin this for me."

"I wouldn't. Don't forget it took me several run-ins with Ally before she agreed to go out with me."

"That's right. How could I forget? I heard the story from both sides. It started at Joe's Café, right?"

"Yep, she ran right into me, literally, and I knew then and there I was going to find a way to her heart."

"Bro, have you started writing for Hallmark?"

"Sorry, Ally makes me sappy sometimes."

"You going to ask her to marry you?"

"Bro. Too soon. Now you sound like Mom." We both laugh.

"Sorry. Speaking of Mom. How's it going?"

"It's fine. Tom says the basement's almost done, and then you and I will have to go put all the furniture back in place. Have I mentioned I'm glad you're back? It wasn't always easy when you weren't here."

"I know. I apologized to Mom and should apologize to you, too. Sorry. I just couldn't stay."

"I understand. It all worked out in the end. And now you're here to help me move furniture," Oliver jokes, lightening the mood.

"Yep, and I'm meeting Morgan at Joe's tomorrow, so maybe that's a good omen."

"Good luck."

"Thanks."

"Later, bud."

"Later, Olly."

I hang up the phone and get ready for bed.

The next morning, I meet Morgan at Joe's for breakfast.

"I'll have a mocha latte and a ham and cheese croissant," Morgan orders when it's our turn.

"I'll have a black coffee with the egg bites," I order, then pay for both of us.

"Hot bean water? Do you hate yourself?" Morgan teases as we move to the pickup counter.

I laugh at her description. "I will be adding cream and sweetener to it. I just don't want all the syrupy junk in it," I assure her.

"Okay good, I was afraid this date would be over before it got started."

"I thought we agreed this wasn't a date?" I raise a brow in question.

"No, you said it wasn't, but I put it on my calendar, so yes, it is." She nods and thanks the girl behind the counter for her order.

"I see. I've never had a shopping date before. In total

transparency, I hate to go shopping," I admit, sheepishly as we take a seat by the window and remove our coats.

"Are you serious? Why did you agree to go?" she asks in surprise, blowing on her coffee before taking a sip.

"To spend more time with you." I see her expression soften at those words, and I hope she knows it's not just a line.

She sits upright and looks me in the eye then raises her right hand. "I, Morgan Pierce, do solemnly promise to make sure you have a good time. I know what works and what doesn't, so there will be no try-on montages set to music with me. We'll get in and get out." She puts her hand down, picks up her croissant, and takes a bite.

"Morgan Pierce, I accept your solemn vow." I pop an egg bite in my mouth and then add the cream and sweetener to my coffee.

"It'll be fun. You're in good hands."

"I seem to remember those talented hands," I flirt.

"They do know a thing or two." She blows on her fingernails then rubs them on her sweater as if polishing them.

"That they do. Is there a scenario that would get us back to that situation in the future," I venture to ask and almost want to take it back immediately until I hear her answer.

"I'd say there are many scenarios possible that would lead to that conclusion, and I'm agreeable to seeing which scenario is best," she answers, and I get a little twitch below the belt. "Full transparency, I like hanging out with you and would be agreeable to doing it as often as our schedules allow."

"Maybe we should wait for you to say that until after you take me shopping. You may change your mind."

"Fair enough. I'll submit my verdict at the end of the day," she continues in a playful voice.

We finish our meals and gather our belongings for the trek out into the cold.

"First stop, Harry's Outdoor Mart for a coat!" Morgan cheers as we step outside.

"Where?"

"Just kidding. I'm taking you to Finley's first. You brought your credit card, right?" She grabs my jacket and pulls me behind her. I pat my pocket to make sure my wallet is there and hurry to catch up to walk beside her.

I find a much warmer coat at Finley's. It is a *hazel*, not brown, wool car coat with an added layer underneath so I look more *put together* than if I were just wearing a puffer coat. We pick out matching gloves and a scarf, and I wear it out of the store.

We only go to two other stores because Morgan was right: she knew exactly what to get. I picked out the colors I liked from the items she chose. I tried them on, they fit perfectly, and we checked out. She said my spring wardrobe may require the tailoring she mentioned as a warning in advance of our next shopping trip. We're done by lunch and as we walk to the *cute*—her word—French café she found, we pass a women's clothing store and I pull her in.

"Pick something for yourself for helping me today."

"Really? I don't really need anything."

"I thought girls could always find a reason to shop. How about this?" I hold out a hot pink scarf that matches the blush on her cheeks from the cold air.

"I love it. It's my favorite color. Thank you."

I nod and hand it to the saleswoman. After I pay for it, I wrap it around her neck and give her a quick peck on the lips.

"I'm having a good time," she sighs as I pull away.

"Me too. Let's get some lunch." I take her hand and squeeze it as I lead her to the café.

The place is casual and painted in pink and black paint, but they still have linen tablecloths. We order our food at the counter, and they let us know they'll bring it to the table when it's ready.

"I have to admit, shopping wasn't as painful as I thought it would be," I start once we're seated at a small two-top table toward the back.

"It's not when you have me by your side. It was fun," she says, removing her scarf.

"I thought it would take much longer."

"You made out really well and you have a common

size, so it was easy to find things. You did take things in stride, so I feel I can disclose my verdict … I am agreeable to another date with you."

"I accept your verdict. Do you have any plans for the rest of the day?" I ask.

"Not really. I thought this would be an all-day event and didn't plan anything else." She throws her hands up in a shrug.

"Would you like to come back to my place and hang out?"

"Yes. I admit that I'm not ready to go home yet."

"I'm glad." I take her hand and hold it until our food arrives.

"This tomato soup is really good," Morgan states after taking a taste.

I taste mine. "It's smooth and the hint of spice gives it a nice flavor," I agree.

"I've never been here. We'll have to remember this place."

"I like that," I say, holding my spoon in mid-air.

"What?"

"When you use the word 'we' in a sentence," I clarify before bringing the spoon to my mouth.

"Me too. I could get used to it."

I hold out my spoon and we clink ours together as we cheer to our successful day. I smile and continue to eat. Morgan seems to be okay with spending more time with me, and I couldn't be happier. Once we're done eating, a woman comes to clear our plates. I leave a tip for her, and then we gather the bags and our coats and take a very warm cab back to my apartment.

❄

AFTER I LET her in the door, I take her coat and hang it up as we kick off our shoes then take my bags back to my room. I don't hear her follow me and almost run into her when I turn around to go back to the kitchen.

"Oh, sorry. I didn't hear you."

"That's okay. I wasn't sure if I should wait or follow you."

"I was going to grab us drinks and then have us come in here anyway. Since I don't have a living room, I just watch shows on my laptop on my bed. Are you okay with that? If not, we can go to your place," I rush out, worried she's going to bolt.

"That's perfect. I would love to get under some covers. I'm still thawing out." Morgan crosses her arms and rubs her hands up and down them to warm up.

"I'll turn up the heat. What can I get you to drink? I have water, iced tea, hot tea."

"Any chance you have hot chocolate?" Morgan asks.

"Let me check. Mom might have stocked that because she often likes to drink it before bed."

Morgan follows me to the kitchen, and I check the cabinets. Sure enough, there is some hot chocolate. I grab two packets.

"Is skim milk okay?"

"Sure. My grandma used to make it with whole milk, and it was my favorite. I'll take any milk over hot water."

"Perfect." I heat up the milk in a pan on the stove and add the cocoa when it comes to a boil then stir.

"How long do you think you'll have the gym in here?" Morgan asks, looking over the equipment.

"A little longer than I'd like. The AC died in the other gym, so once I make the money back that I spent to replace it, I can start looking."

"That sucks. This space is going to be amazing when it can be a living room. I mean, that wall is perfect for a big-screen TV. Although you may have to get some room darkening shades if you watch anything during the day with all the sunlight coming in through your large windows."

I turn from the stove to pour the hot cocoa into two mugs and place hers on the counter in front of her.

"I agree. I've had some ideas for the space, but it would be nice to have your expertise when I go shopping for furniture."

"I'm your girl!" She cheers and clinks her cup against mine. *Apparently, that's our thing now, we clink.*

"I like the sound of that."

She sobers when she realizes what she just said. "I

mean, you know what I mean, I'll be available to help you shop," she stammers.

"Right. My personal shopper girl. Got it." I nod and take a sip of the hot chocolate. "Ready to go watch a movie? We can take the rest into my room."

"Sure." She slides off the bar stool and follows me.

I set her mug on the side table, pull back the covers for her to tuck in, and then hand her back the mug.

"Thank you. Your bed is so comfortable." She sighs and wiggles into the pillows I set up against the headboard.

"Yeah, I wasn't leaving it behind in California. It took me forever to find one I liked." I pull back the covers on my side and jump in. Then I grab my laptop from the drawer of the side table and open it up. "What would you like to watch?"

"Have you seen, *Keeping Up with the Joneses*?" she asks.

"Yes. It's hilarious. It's one of my favorites." I start scrolling through my list of movies.

"Me too. And don't get me started on Jon Hamm."

"Don't get *me* started on Gal Gadot."

"Oh, for sure, she's hot," Morgan agrees, shocking the hell out of me.

"Wow, most girls I've met wouldn't admit that."

"Yeah, well, I can admit when someone's hot. Facts are facts." She laughs, and I think I like her even more.

I put the movie on, and she snuggles into my shoulder. I take a few shallow breaths to calm myself because I don't want her to see how much I love having her in my bed and curled into my side. Once we start laughing together, my nerves subside.

I'm not sure when I fell asleep, but when I wake my neck is kinked from sleeping in an upright position without a pillow and Morgan is no longer at my side but scooched down with her head in my lap. I carefully lift her head and move down to rest my head on my pillow. Then I tuck her into my side and quickly fall back to sleep.

After a few hours, Morgan startles awake and lifts her head from my shoulder and looks around like she's not sure where she is.

"Hey there, sleepyhead," I whisper.

"Wow. I can't believe I fell asleep on you. I'm so sorry. We didn't even shop that much." She pushes her hair out of her face and tucks it behind her ear.

"It's fine. I think it's because I turned up the heat and it just knocked us both out. I guess we needed it."

"I guess so."

"What time is it?" She squints and looks at the window as if trying to gauge the hour.

"It's about five."

"I better get going." She stands and smooths out her clothes.

"You don't have to. We can order in some dinner. Finish out the day."

"That sounds nice, but I think I'll pick something up at the market and head home. My brain is still a little groggy."

"If that's what you want, I'll walk you out." We grab our mugs and walk them out to the kitchen sink.

"I have a busy week coming up, so I won't be around much until the weekend," Morgan states while putting on her shoes.

"Is that your way of telling me not to expect to hear from you until our date next weekend?"

"Yes, but know that I'll be looking forward to seeing you," she says, lifting her coat from the hook.

"Why don't you think about where you want to go and let me know," I offer.

"Okay, I will. Thanks for breakfast and lunch and the scarf and hot cocoa," she rattles off as I help her into her coat.

"You're welcome. Thank you for styling me." I wrap my arms around her from behind and whisper in her ear, "Full transparency. I wish you were staying." I release her and she turns and puts her hand on my chest. "Full transparency. I'm willing to try this dating scenario to get to the part where I stay." She places a kiss on my cheek.

"I am agreeable to that scenario." I lean down and kiss her on the lips. Without another word, she leaves my apartment and walks down the steps. I watch until I hear the door close at the bottom of the stairs.

CHAPTER ELEVEN
Morgan

I'M STILL IN a lust-induced stupor when I get in the shower on Monday morning. The fortress around my heart took another hit when Tyler bought me the scarf. It was a sweet gesture of gratitude, and it meant a lot to me. I didn't have the words to describe my time with Tyler to Ally, so I kept the feelings to myself and spent all day yesterday doing laundry, picking out my outfit for work, and finally reading my Oliver Hudson book.

If today weren't *the* Monday of all Mondays, I'd call in sick to finish it. It's that good. I only put it down so I wouldn't have dark circles under my eyes when I met *the* Tanya LeBoux. When her name flashes in my brain, I turn up the rock music on my waterproof speaker and dance and sing out all the excitement so I can remain professional when I get to the office. The neighbors will just have to deal with the noise this morning. After my hair and makeup are done, I walk to my closet where my outfit is hanging on the door.

I knew I would need to wear something that allowed me to easily move around the studio yet still look like I knew about fashion, so I settled on a loose, silky, pale-pink blouse with a bow at the neck and flowy, straight-legged, black dress pants that will move with me if I need to squat or stretch in different positions.

When I'm finished getting ready, I grab my coat, messenger bag, and travel mug and head out the door. Once I'm on the sidewalk, I call Ally.

"Hi, Bestie! Good morning. How are you doing on this lovely day?" I sing into the phone when she answers.

"I'm great, and it sounds like you are too. Did you have another good weekend with Tyler?"

"Yes, I did! We went shopping and then we agreed to another date."

"What?! I feel we're going to need more than a ten-minute debrief on this," Ally says sarcastically.

"We will, I promise. But the bullet points are that I realized that I shouldn't fight this. That I should take a chance on Tyler. Plus, if we date, we can also do other things that we did once but aren't currently doing."

"Morgan! You're terrible. But I gotta admit, if he's half as good as Oliver ..." Ally trails off.

"Ally focus. That's not the only good thing. This is my big week."

"That's right. It's Tanya week! Woohoo!" Ally cheers.

"I can't even believe this in my life now. Just a few weeks ago I was crying in my Cheerios about my dead-end job and non-existent love life and look at me now!"

"I'm so happy for you Morgan! You'll have to tell me everything when you get home."

"I will. Gotta run!"

"Good luck, bestie. You've got this!"

"Thank you!"

I end the call and make my way into the building and to my new office with a spring in my step.

❄

AS ALANA, ELLIOT, and I patiently wait for Tanya to arrive I must admit that Elliot and I did a terrific job with this setup. Several *very* attractive men are stationed in the different areas we created around the makeshift gym. They're dressed in the provided workout wear, ready to pose for Tanya's final say. At that thought the nerves kick in, and I cross my legs and nervously shake my foot. What if she doesn't like the setup? The men we've brought in? Me? I'm about to jump out of my skin when Alana gets a text that Tanya just arrived.

Our temporary 'me' replacement ushers her into the studio, and she sparkles with a kind of glow you can only get in California. She is tall, tan, and mesmerizing. There's not a golden lock of hair out of place or a wrinkle in her cream-colored silk clothing. She is breathtaking. Almost angelic. I can tell you that the red-carpet photos don't do her justice.

"Hello, Tanya. It's good to see you again," Alana greets Tanya with a two-handed handshake.

"Alana! You look beautiful as ever! I'm so happy to be back. I was so pleased with the women's line layout."

"We're happy you're back. Unfortunately, Carolyn won't be your lead this time, but I've put you in good hands. Let me introduce you to Morgan." Alana leads Tanya in my direction, and I dart my eyes to Elliot and discretely wipe my palms on my pants as I stand.

"Morgan, meet Tanya LeBoux. Tanya this is Morgan. She is extremely organized and has an amazing attention to detail. I think you will be pleased with her work," Alana introduces.

"Morgan! What a cute top. I love it," Tanya compliments before pulling me into a hug. "It's so nice to meet you."

"Thank you. It's an honor to work with you," I reply as we step apart and Elliot comes to my side.

"And you remember Elliot," Alana adds.

"Oh gosh, yes. Elliot. How are you?" Tanya asks, pulling him in for a hug.

"Fabulous as ever," he replies with a little hip swivel.

"I believe it. You look terrific."

"You know me. I'm always dressed in the latest fashions," he says.

"A man after my own heart," Tanya agrees.

"Everyone is ready. As you can see, we've brought in several models for you to choose from. We've given them their poses for each station. Are you ready?" Alana says, bringing everyone back to the task at hand.

"Oh my gosh. Did you not get my message?" Tanya gasps, wide-eyed, covering her mouth with her hand.

"No, I didn't. When did you send it?" Alana is feverishly tapping on her iPad.

"Last week. Maybe I accidentally sent it to Jonathan. I'm sorry you did all this work and that we have to pay for all these models. I wanted to let you know I had already picked my brand ambassador and would be bringing him with me."

Alana stops looking at her iPad and looks at Tanya in shock. I'm fidgeting with my hands, and Elliot is taking everything in stride with a look of excitement on his face like he's about to open a birthday present. Not at all like he'd spent hours picking out the models that are now of no use.

"Okay. Morgan, please escort these men out and let them know they will be compensated for their time. Tanya, let's get your guy in here and start staging the shots and check the lighting," Alana instructs without skipping a beat. I nod and do as she says.

"Gentlemen, there has been a change of plans. Ms.

LeBoux decided to go in a different direction. Will you follow me?" I announce as I corral the men out the door and toward the changing room. "You all will still be compensated for your time. Thank you for coming." I get a few disappointed looks, a few nods of understanding, and one inappropriate wink before heading back into the studio.

I can't imagine who Tanya picked to be her brand ambassador, and I wonder if it's another famous celebrity. *Does she know Stephen Amell?* I momentarily imagine his *Arrow* training scenes then laugh to myself and hurry back to the studio.

When I enter the room Alana, Tanya, and Elliot have formed a semi-circle around the mystery model, who is sitting at the bench press, as they give him instructions for the first pose. I start to join them when they step back and call for our photographer, Simon. As the model rises my jaw drops. Standing before me, in all his golden glory, is *my* Tyler Hudson. Tyler's eyes go wide when he sees me, and my legs give out. He makes a move toward me, but I hold up my hand and quickly grab onto the weight rack to keep myself from joining my jaw on the floor. He stops and I recognize the look of concern on his face because it matches mine. Alana, Tanya, and Elliot all turn to look at me. I take a deep breath and join them.

"Ah, Morgan, terrific timing. This is Tyler Hudson.

He's a good friend of Tanya's. You and Elliot will be working closely with him on this shoot. Just have him go through the poses today and we'll get started tomorrow. We're going to leave you to it. Let me know if you have any questions, but the required shots have been shared with you, and it should be an easy day," Alana says before guiding Tanya out the door.

"Bye, everyone." Tanya wiggles her fingers as a wave and exits.

"Hey, I thought you said you were staying with me," Tyler calls to Tanya.

"You'll be in good hands. Just do what Morgan tells you. I need to talk to Jonathan while I'm here," she replies and walks out the door.

I straighten my back and turn to Tyler. "Mr. Hudson. It's a pleasure to have you," I say, my eyes pleading with him to keep his mouth shut about us.

"Morgan, was it?" Tyler asks with a grin.

"Yes. Morgan Pierce. Can we get you to stand here?" I ask, pulling him into the light.

"I get the feeling that they aren't supposed to know about us," Ty whispers.

"Yes, Mr. Hudson. That's it. Stand here," I assert. He gives me a brief nod.

I continue in my most professional manner because I am standing in front of my new lover at my new job and I'm afraid I'm not going to be able to keep both.

CHAPTER TWELVE
Tyler

I KNEW ABOUT Morgan's new job, but she never told me she'd be working on Tanya's account, and I don't know why. She knew we were friends. I could have talked her up to Tanya. Now I'm standing here, posing, and she's acting like we don't know each other. I'm taking her lead, but it's hard to not touch her, hug her, or tease her. She's like a completely different person, and I'm trying to figure out what's going on.

After walking through the poses, she offers me a bottle of water.

"Can I get you anything else Mr. Hudson?" she asks.

"The water's fine. Are we done for today? It'd be nice if I could get a few clients in this afternoon. I'm a personal trainer by day, and I guess, now I can say model too," I cheekily explain as if she doesn't know me.

"Lighting looks good on the sample shots. I'd say we're done here," the photographer says.

"Thank you, Simon. I'll see you tomorrow," Morgan

dismisses him, and he saunters out of the room.

"Anything else you need from me?" Elliot asks Morgan, giving me a once-over.

"Yes, can you make sure everyone is confirmed for tomorrow? Makeup, caterers, outfits? I'll reset the props before I leave," Morgan replies, brushing off her pants and walking over to pick up a dumbbell.

"Sure thing." Elliot makes a few notes on his iPad and quickly walks out of the room.

"Can we talk about this?" I ask. Morgan whips her head up at me and her eyes go wide then dart around the room making sure we're alone. Then I notice her twitch her head to the door. I slowly rise, and as I suspiciously follow her to the door, I'm suddenly pushed into a storage closet. "Whoa, what are you doing?" I ask in shock.

"Shh, be quiet," she says, closing the door behind us, causing our bodies to touch within the confines of the clutter.

"Is this some sort of role play?" I ask. She smacks my chest.

"No. Keep your voice down. You are going to get me in trouble," she whispers. The scent of her perfume makes me want to take her up against the door, but I remain quiet and still. "As a requisite of this position, we are not allowed to fraternize with the models. I could lose my job." She tries to wave her arms around but accidentally knocks over a mop. The noise causes her to cover my mouth to keep me from speaking while she holds her breath. No one comes to check out the noise and she continues. "Oh, thank God no one heard that. Now we will go out there and act like we don't know each other. Do you understand me?"

Her hand is still over my mouth, so I nod in agreement.

"Thank you," she whispers out with a huff.

She carefully cracks open the door to make sure we are still alone. Once she confirms the coast is clear we exit the closet, and we stand face to face.

"It was a pleasure working with you, Ms. Pierce." I slightly bow before sidestepping her and silently walking out of the room.

※

I HAD NO idea what to expect but after the walkthrough today, I'm sure everything will go smoothly tomorrow. I make a few calls on my way home to let a few clients know I can fit them in this afternoon since we were done early.

After the sessions, I tidy up the gym, wipe everything down, then strip off my workout gear and hit the shower. As I'm rinsing the shampoo from my hair, I hear a loud banging on my door. I quickly finish, hop out of the shower, and wrap a towel around my waist as I slip-slide out of the bathroom. I check the peephole and see Morgan about to pound on the door again and pull open the door. With her momentum, she falls into my arms, and I catch her with a kiss.

"What was that?" she asks, pushing off me all flustered.

"I couldn't resist. It was hard pretending I didn't know you today," I admit, taking her hand and guiding her out of the doorway. "Come in and tell me what's going on."

She takes a seat on a barstool, inhales deeply, then lets out a huge sigh. "My boss told me that sometimes we get models who get handsy and if they are, they are fired immediately. So, if they can't flirt with us, we can't flirt with them. I can't let them know we're together. I can't flirt with you, and you can't touch me either. We'll both get fired."

"I'm not going to get fired. Tanya would never fire me. I'm not one of your typical models, so I don't think the rules apply to me or to you," I say in my most calming voice.

"Tyler, this is my first assignment in my new position. I can't mess this up. You already have a successful business, I don't. I want a better life for myself, and it starts with a better-paying job."

"Let me talk to Tanya."

"No. Don't." She holds up her hand. "I want to do this on my own."

"Morgan, let me help you. You're wigging out."

"I am not." She plants a hand on her hip. "Will you please just go with it?"

I hold my hands up in defeat.

"Fine. We'll do it your way."

She pauses and looks me in the eye. "Do you promise to be on your best behavior?"

"I promise. I'll do my best for you. Now come give me a hug. I had a hard time keeping my hands off you today."

Morgan stands and walks into my arms. I hold her until I can feel her energy start to calm down.

"Should we go tell Oliver and Ally about our day?" Morgan asks. "I promised I'd call her when I got home and since I'm already here, I might as well talk to her in person."

"Sure. Let me get some clothes on and I'll be right over." Morgan laughs.

"That's probably a good idea. Plus, the less time I see you like this," she wiggles her finger up and down as her eyes rove over my body, "the easier it will be to pretend I've never met you before."

Now it's my turn to laugh. "I'll meet you over there."

Morgan gives me a quick kiss and runs out the door.

CHAPTER THIRTEEN
Morgan

ALLY IS SURPRISED to see me when I knock on her door.

"Hey, what are you doing here?"

"You will not believe what happened today," I say, pushing my way through the door and straight to her couch.

"Do we need wine or ice cream?" she asks.

"Wine."

"On it," she calls from the kitchen. I kick off my shoes and get comfortable while she brings out the wine. Once she's set everything down on the table and poured the wine, I sit on the edge of the couch and reach for my glass. "Now spill!" she demands while I casually take a sip of wine.

"You will not believe who Tanya picked to be the model for her men's line."

"Who?" There's a knock on the door, and Ally looks between me and the door. "Hold that thought," she says, rising from the couch.

"Hey, Allison."

"Tyler. Come in. Morgan was just starting to tell me about her day. Want a glass of wine?"

"Sure," Tyler says, coming to sit next to me while Ally diverts to the kitchen for another glass.

"So, who did Tanya pick to be the model? Is it a celebrity? Am I going to hate you for life?" Ally asks, returning with a glass for Tyler then picking hers back up to take a sip.

"I don't think so," I say with a giggle.

"Well, who is it?" Ally shouts impatiently, almost spilling her wine.

"Me," Tyler states.

"What? How?" Ally stutters, looking between the two of us.

"I train Tanya LeBoux in California and we've become friends. She asked me to be her brand ambassador for the men's line. When Morgan told us about her job the other night, I never put two and two together," Tyler explains.

"Well, that's awesome. Knowing the model has got to be an advantage, right?" Ally says before taking a sip of wine.

"Wrong," I say with a pout. "Remember how I told you just this morning that Tyler and I were officially dating?"

"Yeah?" Ally says nervously, putting her glass down on the table.

"Well, now we can't."

"Why are you dragging this out? Will you just get to the point?" Ally says in exasperation.

"In my position, I'm not allowed to date the models, and since Tyler is now a model, we can't date," I finally get out.

"Oh."

"I told her I'd just explain to Tanya that we were dating before we knew the rules, but she won't let me," Tyler adds.

"I don't want special treatment. I want to prove myself first," I defend.

"I see. What if we all go out on a group date or what about the bar hops?" Ally questions as if trying to find a loophole.

"I guess in a group would be fine," I admit. "And hopefully this will all be over by the Christmas party hop and it won't matter who I'm dating."

"Okay, well, if it were me, I'd just be up-front with them so I wouldn't have to sneak around," Ally says.

"Well, that's you. You and Tyler, and even Oliver, already have successful careers. I don't. I've always wanted to work in fashion. This is literally a dream come true, and I'm not about to mess it up for some guy," I confidently explain.

"I see," Tyler says, looking defeated.

"I'm sorry Tyler." I rub his arm. "You're a great guy. I know I agreed to this dating thing, but I can't jeopardize my career for it. If you can wait for me, I'd appreciate it. If you find someone else and move on, I'll understand."

"Morgan, wait. Let's not go jumping off into the deep end." Tyler places his hand on my arm. "I would like to see where this goes. I enjoy spending time with you. I'm still getting started here, so I definitely can wait. And the best part is that we still get to see each other," Tyler calmly states and immediately puts me at ease.

"Thank you."

He sits back on the couch with his wine, and I curl into him. We try to come up with a game plan with Ally, but our scenarios go from bad to worse as we drink our wine, and we all end up in hysterics.

We decide to order some dinner and after we're done, I head home to prep for what I'm sure will be a very interesting photo shoot.

❄

WHEN MY ALARM goes off, I crawl out of bed and take a shower. As I stand under the water, I pray that Ty and I can keep it together today. Once I'm dressed, I pad to the kitchen to make coffee, but there's a knock at the door. I check the peephole and see that it's Tyler.

"What are you doing here?" I ask when I open the door.

"Brought you breakfast," he says holding up coffee and a paper bag.

"Aw, that's so sweet." *Fortress hit number three.* "And you're right on time. I was just about to make my coffee to go."

"Oh good. You can eat real quick, and then I'll walk you to work. Now that I have my new coat, I don't mind walking as much."

"You look great in it," I admit, taking him in for the first time. "But you can't walk me to work," I say, taking the coffee and bagel from him. He unzips his coat but leaves it on while we sit at my kitchen table to eat.

"Right. You look beautiful by the way. Almost too good. Don't you have a trash bag or something you can wear over that top so I'm not distracted all day?" Tyler teases.

"Thank you. And no, I don't. I need to look good. I thought skinny, stretchy pants would work best with all the moving around we have to do today."

"And that tight top shows off your assets." He waggles his brows.

"What assets? There's practically nothing there." I look down and wave over my chest.

"Hey, hey, don't diss the girls. I happen to like them

very much." I laugh and swat at him and his bulging eyes that are fixed on my chest.

"What if I walk you to that café right before your office building?"

I roll my eyes up to the ceiling to think then look back at Ty. "That could work. Thank you."

"You're welcome. I want to spend what time I can with you."

"Full transparency. I do too."

"Good," Ty says, giving me a kiss on the cheek.

"Let me get my coat and we can go." I throw the trash away and then grab my bag, coat, and coffee. Once I lock up, we head out to the sidewalk.

We part ways at the café as if we're just two random people walking down the street next to each other so no one knows we're a couple. When I get to the office, I have a message to meet everyone in the studio, so I drop my bag under my desk and walk down there. When I enter, Simon and Henry are positioning the lights and Elliot is flirting with the catering manager. I walk to the food table to introduce myself.

"Hi, I'm Morgan. Thank you for being here."

"Will. Nice to meet you. I think we're just about ready."

"Great. If you need anything else let either me or Elliot know."

"Thank you. I will." He winks at Elliot.

"Elliot, since Will has all this handled, can you start preparing the outfits and make sure they are in order of the list Tanya sent? It's in the shared folder."

He drops his head in disappointment but quickly hands the manager his card and does as I ask. I have a feeling we just made a love match. Technically, he isn't a model, so I guess he's fair game. I shrug to myself and am about to continue setting up when Alana comes into the room.

"Everything looks great Morgan."

"Thank you. I was just about to do a walk-through before Mr. Hudson and Tanya arrive." She looks at her watch.

"You are right on time as I knew you would be. You're doing a terrific job. The food looks delicious. I'm so glad you found that new place for us. I did *not* enjoy the cold eggs and dry baked goods last time," she admits, tucking her chin and raising her brow.

"Everything is low carb and high protein today. I thought that would be best for a fitness shoot."

"You thought correctly."

I smile at the compliments. Alana is happy, and I'm elated.

"Since you seem to have everything under control, I need to meet with Jonathan before Tanya gets here."

"Okay. Mr. Hudson should be here at nine. I'll give him time to settle in and then we'll get started."

"I knew you were the perfect candidate for the job." Alana clasps her hands in satisfaction and then turns to exit but stops and addresses the room. "Everyone. Could I have your attention for just a moment?" Everyone stops what they are doing and focuses on her. "Morgan is in charge. If you have any issues or questions, see her first. You are in capable hands, and I expect this to go off without a hitch." Everyone murmurs and nods in agreement and then the room erupts into a flurry of activity as Alana confidently strides out of the room. I so want to be her when I grow up.

Once everyone is ready to get started, I invite them all to the food table to have a little social time before the work begins. We're all chatting away and making jokes when Ty walks in.

I notice him and it's like those slow-motion shots in movies where the hot guy strides across the room to kiss the girl and gives the camera a little head flip. My mouth waters at the sight of him, but when Simon barks out a laugh next to me, I'm quickly brought back to the moment and call Tyler over.

CHAPTER FOURTEEN
Tyler

I WALK INTO the café and Morgan keeps walking to work. I stare out the window until she's out of sight and then order a coffee and have a seat by the window. I decide to call Oliver and give him an update.

"Hey man, what's up?" Oliver asks when he answers.

"Nothing much. Just waiting to go to my modeling gig."

"What?"

I laugh at his confusion. "Tanya came out with some workout clothes and wants to release a men's line and asked me to model for her."

"When did all this happen?"

"That week you did the reading. Guess who I'm working with?"

"If you say Scarlett Johansson we are no longer brothers." I chuckle at the suggestion of his actress crush.

"Nope. Morgan."

"I thought she was a receptionist or something?"

Oliver questions.

"Oh, that's right, you hadn't gotten to the diner yet when she told us she got promoted. This is her first photo shoot."

"That's awesome. I'm sure you'll work well together."

"You sound like Allison. But it's not awesome. They can't know we're dating."

"Why not?"

"Something about not fraternizing with the clients. I told her I'd talk to Tanya but it's a no-go for her."

"So basically, telling you that you can't do something makes you want it even more, right?"

"You know it."

"You can't get her fired," Oliver warns.

"I know. It's just hard to keep my hands to myself after she finally agreed to date me."

"You can and you will," Oliver bosses. I take a deep breath in and let it out slowly.

"How's Mom? Are you two surviving?" I ask, changing the subject because thoughts of Morgan in my bed just invaded my mind and I can't think about that today.

"Yep!" I can hear the smile in his voice and know something's up.

"What did you do with her?"

"IIIII ... took her home," he cheers.

"The house is done?"

"Yep! She's back home and happy as a clam. Now I can write in peace and stop throwing darts at your headshot that I have pinned to my dart board."

"Not cool, bro."

"It's what I do when I have writer's block." He laughs. "I'm just teasing. Everything is fine. She didn't bother me too much, and my apartment is spotless." Now it's my turn to laugh.

"My gym equipment is still shiny after two weeks of clients," I add, agreeing that our mom's cleaning talents are unmatched. I check my watch.

"Oh man, I gotta run."

"Okay, let me know how it goes. Hopefully you'll be wearing more than you do for your bodybuilding competitions."

"This is workout wear, not competition wear. But you might be on to something. I'll have to talk to her about that," I say with a laugh.

"Please don't," Olly pleads before disconnecting.

I toss my cup and head to Morgan's office.

❅

I'M ESCORTED INTO the studio at nine a.m., on the dot, to a team of people chatting around the food table. A quick look around the room suddenly makes this all very real, and I realize I'm not prepared for it. There are lights in different positions all around the room. There's a makeup station with paintbrushes. Next to that station is a barber-style chair in front of a mirror with a hairdryer, a long stick thing, and then something that looks like what I think is called a straightener. Lined up along the bottom of the mirror are more bottles of hair products than I've ever seen or used in my whole life. I'm about to turn and tell Tanya that I can't do this when Morgan spots me and calls me over to the food table.

"Mr. Hudson, good morning. Please come have some coffee and some food. Then I can introduce you to your team," Morgan greets.

"Thank you. I forgot to have my shake this morning."

"Take as much as you'd like, we have plenty."

I plate some eggs and fruit and stand awkwardly while she introduces me to Simon's assistant Henry, Melanie, the makeup artist, and Victoria, the hairstylist. And of course, I remember Elliot. I'm instantly relieved when Tanya glides in with a flourish."

"Tyler. There's my hunky model. Are you ready? If this goes well, I could make you my next leading man," she cheers in excitement.

"Slow down Tanya. I've already told you that's not the life for me. I like what I do."

"A girl can dream," she sighs then addresses Morgan. "What do we have here?"

"We have a wide variety of high protein, low carb breakfast options and we'll have salads and grilled meat options for lunch," Morgan explains with pride.

Tanya claps in glee. "Oh, thank you so much. I'm so hungry, and I hate when there's nothing for me to eat on set." She quickly grabs a plate and starts with the egg bites and ends with a spoonful of fruit. Her plate does not look like the plate of someone who is starving, but I know she tends to cut back more when she's not working out with me as often. She gives me a look asking for my approval and I nod. She smiles and takes a bite of the eggs.

"Wow, these are so light and fluffy and not rubbery. Morgan, I'm going to have to get the name of this caterer."

"Sure thing. I have all our service providers on a list that I can forward to you. I'll send it now." Morgan taps her iPad and sends it off to Tanya.

"Perfect."

Tanya finishes her food and tosses her plate into the trash can while everyone gets into position. Morgan walks the room and makes sure everyone is doing what they are supposed to do.

"You ready for this? I know it was a lot of me to ask of you," Tanya says, rubbing my arm.

"I think so. I wasn't prepared to see a hair and makeup team though." She giggles and keeps rubbing my arm. Just then Morgan looks over and I can see her eyes focus on Tanya's hand. She quickly looks back at what Simon is showing her, and I step away from Tanya, causing her hand to drop.

"Is something wrong?" Tanya asks, with a look of concern.

"No. It's just that I heard that the models can't fraternize with the staff. I don't want anyone to get the wrong impression of us."

She rubs my arm again. "Don't be silly. I'm Tanya LeBoux, I can do as I please. You're like family and we're friends." She waves her arms for emphasis.

"Yeah, but if you keep rubbing my arm like that, they will think we're more than that." My eyes dart around the room, but no one is currently looking at us.

"I didn't realize I was doing it, and I'm sorry I made you uncomfortable," Tanya apologizes and removes her hand.

"I don't care how we act in the gym because it's my territory, but this is Morgan's first shoot and I want to be on my best behavior."

"First shoot?"

"You didn't know?" *Shit.*

"No. Alana just said I wouldn't have my normal contact and that she was good, but I had no idea my project was in the hands of an amateur!" Tanya is visibly upset, and I need to make this right and fast.

I grab both of her arms and she gives me a look of *who's touching who now*, but I continue.

"Don't say anything. I'm sure Morgan will do a good job. Give her a chance, and if she doesn't live up to your expectations, then you can say something." Tanya's face softens and then she smiles.

"We all deserve our big break, don't we?"

I know she had a highly regarded actress vouch for her when she started and she skyrocketed to stardom.

"Yes, we do. Thank you."

"Why do you care so much about this Morgan person anyway?" She squints her eyes at me. I shrug feigning nonchalance.

"No reason."

"Tyyyyler."

"Seriously. No reason. I just like to give everyone a chance. You know me. I always want people to succeed."

"Uh, huh. I don't know what you're hiding, but I'll let it go for now."

"Nothing."

She gives me a quizzical look of disbelief when I'm mercifully saved by Elliot.

"Mr. Hudson, I need you to come with me to change into your first outfit," he says, gesturing toward a door next to the beauty stations.

"Looks like I gotta get started. Talk to you later Tanya." I shrug and follow Elliot.

"Oh, we will." She gives me one last I'm-going-to-get-to-the-bottom-of-this look as I turn away from her.

Once I'm dressed in the first outfit, which is a camo-green tank and black shorts with a camo strip down the sides, I'm escorted to the makeup chair and then finally the hair station where I'm straightened and gelled into perfection. As I take in my appearance, I have to admit I clean up pretty well. If I didn't have to worry about sweating it off, this foundation stuff could be a game-changer. I laugh to myself, and I let them lead me to the first pose.

CHAPTER FIFTEEN
Morgan

Once Tyler is ready, I pull up the list of poses on my iPad.

"Okay, everyone. We're going to start with some standing poses," I announce and escort Ty over to the area we set up where all the weights and bands are stacked against the wall. Henry makes the final adjustments to the lights and Simon gets started.

"Flex your arm like you're showing off your muscles," Simon instructs.

"Like this?" Tyler asks, lifting his left arm at a right angle making his bicep pop.

"Yes. Now relax your body."

Tyler puts his arm down.

"No. No. Keep the arm up but try not to look so constipated," Simon chides.

Tyler gives me a 'help me' look and I step in.

"Hold on a sec, Simon. Let me get him in place. I know what you want."

I walk over and try to get Ty into position, but he's fighting me.

"This doesn't feel right. What are you doing to me?" he asks, as I yank on his arm.

"I'm trying to pose you. Can you loosen up? Be like a rag doll that I can manipulate. You're too stiff."

"That's one complaint I've never heard before," he flirts.

I quickly dart my eyes and notice Simon and Henry snicker.

"Mr. Hudson, please, just let me get you in position," I say, putting my hands on my hips.

"Tyler." He states, looking me in the eye.

"Excuse me?" I question, trying to pull his arm down again but end up hanging in midair because he won't budge.

"Call me Tyler. If we're going to be working this close. I'd like you to call me by my first name." He says, almost directly in my face as he bends his head down to where I'm hanging.

"Oh. Okay, Tyler, please relax your arm and then get back into position." He lowers his arm and I'm able to return to a standing position.

He shakes it out and then raises it again. Once I'm satisfied with the pose, Simon walks around Tyler, zooming in for close-ups, backing away for wide shots, and walking around him again to capture different angles, the flash going off the whole time.

We move on to the next position, this time with dumbbells. After Ty does a few curls for action shots and then some stills, we move on.

"Okay, now we need to see a reverse curl."

"What's that?" Ty asks, and I think he's being smart with me.

"The reverse curl, you know when you bend at the waist and extend your arms back?" I explain with a questioning voice.

"I'm sorry, I don't know that one. You'll have to show me what you're talking about." He rubs his chin, hiding a grin with his fingers.

I look to Elliot who's fiddling with his collar in concern. I drop my shoulders and walk over to him in defeat. I grab the weight from his hand which causes it and my upper body to plummet to the floor. I'm currently bent at the waist with my butt up in the air. Tyler laughs. I leave the weight where it is, rise, and glare at him. I adjust my blouse and pick up a lighter dumbbell from the rack. I then proceed to bend my knees, while slightly bending forward at the waist, then extend the dumbbell back. Tyler is still watching me as if he's never seen these before.

"Now, do you see what I mean, Mr. Hudson?" I ask, standing and facing him.

"Hmm, I'm not sure. Can you show me again so I

can get it right?" My eyes dart around the room, and now everyone is snickering.

"Of course," I say, trying to remain professional and not lose my cool. I get back into position and repeat the motion.

After a quick glance at Simon, he says, "Oh right! That's a kickback." He playfully slaps his head. "I can't believe I didn't get that when you said reverse curl." I glare at him as I stand.

"My apologies for using the incorrect term," I quip, before returning the weight back on the rack.

Melanie and Victoria giggle at our antics, and I give them a stern look to find something else to do and they quickly turn to straighten up their stations.

We get through the rest of the poses without any more flirting and move on to the next outfit. This one is a red and navy-blue overlapping diamond pattern on the tank and navy shorts.

After a quick water break, Tyler is changed, his makeup and hair are touched up, and we start the poses over again. Tanya told me she wants all the same poses in each outfit so she can pick which outfit she likes with each pose.

"Flex your arm," Simon starts. This time Tyler looks less stiff but still not in his element.

"Hold on, Simon," I interrupt, and he backs away from Ty.

"Mr. Hudson." He grimaces at the formal name, but I continue. "It says in your bio that you are a competitive bodybuilder as well as a personal trainer, correct?"

"Yes," Tyler admits with a curt nod.

"Don't you have to pose to make the muscles pop?"

"Yes," he answers again with the tilt of his head. The look of confusion at my questioning suddenly turns to one of understanding. "Oh, you want me to pretend I'm posing for a show?"

"Yes! Exactly."

"Why didn't you just say so?"

"Why didn't you just do it?" I snap back and quickly realize my mistake. "Sorry, I didn't mean for it to come out like that, I just meant that I thought someone who posed for competition would be more comfortable modeling than you seem to be."

"I'm the only one who is affected by my performance at a competition. This is Tanya's baby, and I don't want to screw it up for her," he admits. Melanie and Victoria let out a sigh and Simon and Henry share a "good grief," under their breaths.

"That's very thoughtful of you. Just try to relax and let's see what happens when you don't overthink and just have fun with it," I encourage.

"Okay. I'll try, but I'm not used to posing with this much clothing on." He winks and I want to deck him. He is making this so difficult for me. And I just got a vision of him in bed with no clothing on and I'm about to say, screw the job and take him on the bench press. I mean, it's not like I don't already know how good he is in bed. *Why did I agree to keep this a secret?* My girlie bits are starting a revolt, and I'm not sure if I can keep my mind and my heart from surrendering to them. *Fortress hits four, five, six.*

"Simon. Go ahead." I step back and fan myself with the flap of my iPad cover, but it doesn't help. Elliot gives me a conspiratorial look that I ignore, and I grab a bottle of water. My hormones and nerves are on fire, and I need to calm down. I can't let my guard down. Tanya might not fire Ty, but I can easily be replaced. I take a sip of water and watch as Tyler moves as if he doesn't have a care in the world. I don't have to make any adjustments, and Simon gets all the shots in record time.

We have enough time to do the third outfit, a black tank with royal blue stitching at the seams and black shorts with the same royal blue piping, before lunch. I can't wait to thank Tyler properly for making the rest of the morning go off without a hitch.

CHAPTER SIXTEEN

Tyler

I'M JUST GETTING into the groove of this modeling gig when Elliot announces that it's time for lunch.

"Great job, everyone. We'll take about an hour break. Please help yourself to as much as you'd like," Morgan announces.

I let out a huge sigh of relief. This modeling business is harder than my toughest workout. I'm relieved this day is half over.

"How many more outfits do I have to do?" I ask Morgan when I join her in line at the buffet table.

"Three more. We're making good time so we might be done early if you keep up the good work!" She fixes herself a grilled chicken salad and adds a dinner roll to her plate.

"I'm doing my best, but I had no idea how tiring this is," I admit, doing the same but leaving the roll since I'm the one in front of the camera.

"Honestly, me either. I kinda wish I could curl up

under my desk and take a nap," she whispers conspiratorially as we take a seat at the round table that's been set up.

"Seriously. Tanya owes me big time. I better have a roster of new clients when I get back to the office."

"So, you guys have always been just friends?"

"Yeah." I'm about to elaborate when Elliot, Simon, and Henry sit down across from us.

"You're doing much better, Tyler," Simon says. "Keep it up."

"Thank you. I was just telling Morgan how tiring this is."

"You'll get used to it," he assures.

"I'll take an Ironman workout any day. I'm glad I don't have to get used to it. I don't plan to continue modeling. I'm just doing a favor for a friend." I emphasize the word friend for Morgan's benefit.

"Dude, how can you just be friends with a hottie like that?" Henry interjects.

"Henry! That's not how we speak about our clients," Morgan scolds.

"Sorry, man, can't help it. She's my favorite actress. I've been a fan since she was in that small indie film before people knew who she was," Henry continues.

"For the record, she came to me as a client and we've had nothing but a professional relationship," I state emphatically to make sure there are no misconceptions with Morgan or any gossipers in the room.

Melanie and Victoria have joined us and I'm not sure who talks to who in this business.

"Got it." Henry nods and then proceeds to stare intently at his salad.

The rest of the group looks every which way but at Morgan and me and starts eating. After a few silent moments, we start the usual banter about the weather and upcoming projects. Once we're finished, I'm escorted back to the dressing room and given a black, short-sleeved tee that ends right at the top of my bicep with a logo in silver over my left pec. And then these long, loose-fitting pants that have a drawstring waist and a silver line down the outside of the legs. I would totally wear these as pajamas. I may steal them when I leave. When I come out, Morgan is there to approve the outfit and then I'm back in the makeup chair, cringing as I now dislike foundation and feel like I'm being smeared with a thick layer of icing on my skin. Then Victoria tousles my hair just so and we start the rotations again.

By the time we're on the final outfit, I've found my groove and Simon keeps clicking away without much comment. I can see why Tanya left this one for last. It's the tightest by far, and I feel like it leaves little to the imagination. There are red and black slashes of color on the tank top and black biker shorts with red slashes all over. *She so owes me. I don't do biker shorts.* I'm very thankful this whole ordeal is just about over.

"And ... done," Simon says, as the last flash of the day pops off.

"I've never been more relieved to hear those words, Simon," I say, sprinting to the changing room. I toss on my sweatpants and the hoodie I arrived in and come back out to a round of applause. I grin and take a bow. "And thank you all for being patient with me," I say to the group with a wave of my arm.

"Great job, Tyler. Simon will get the proofs to us tomorrow and Alana and I will go over them with Tanya. If we need you to come in for a reshoot, I'll call you," Morgan concludes.

"Hey, you finally called me Tyler."

"Well, we're done here so I let it slip," Morgan clarifies.

"Do you think I'll have to come back in?" I cringe.

"Hopefully not, but you never know, it's always a possibility. I guess it really depends on how the model performs." She winks.

"Are you flirting with me, Ms. Pierce?" I cross my arms and flirt back. She darts her eyes and catches Elliot's eyes.

"No. No. Not at all. I-I-didn't mean for it to come out like that," she backpedals.

"No, it's my fault. I shouldn't be unprofessional," I speak up, knowing we got caught.

"It's okay, no harm, Mr. Hudson. Why don't I have Elliot show you out and I'll be in touch if we need anything else."

Elliot comes to stand next to us and I nod in understanding. We're done and therefore can no longer converse. Professional Morgan is back in place.

"You did a terrific job, Mr. Hudson," Elliot states as we walk down the hallway to the front desk. "If I didn't know better, I'd think Ms. Pierce is a little smitten with you."

"Is that so?"

"Yes, I do. I know she's single. You should totally go for it."

"But you guys can't date the models."

"Well, you're done now, aren't you?" He winks.

"I guess that remains to be seen. But I'll keep what you said in mind. I might be a little *smitten* myself," I admit.

"Oh, I'm aware." He laughs then extends his hand. "We'll be in touch, Mr. Hudson."

I shake his hand then he turns and walks back down the corridor.

CHAPTER SEVENTEEN
Morgan

As Elliot and Tyler leave the room I sigh in relief. No more having to pretend that I don't want to jump Ty's bones with every flex, smirk, and smile he shows the camera.

I straighten up the weight equipment while everyone else cleans up their areas.

"Are we leaving everything here tonight?" Melanie asks.

"I think we better in case of any reshoots we might need. I'll let you know sometime tomorrow when you can get your things."

"Okay, then we're off." Melanie and Victoria leave together and pass Elliot in the doorway. They exchange goodbyes with a laugh then Elliot makes a beeline for me.

"So, tell me. Is it just sex or is there more to it?" Elliot asks.

"What?" I ask, almost dropping a hand weight on my

foot but catching it in midair and placing it on the rack.

"Mr. Hudson. Is he a boy *toy* or boy*friend*?" Elliot explains, with a wicked grin on his face.

"Uh, neither. I just met him the other day," I hastily explain, brushing a wayward strand of hair out of my face.

"Nope. Not buying it. Now you're blushing. Something's up with you two," Elliot continues wiggling his index finger up and down in front of me.

"Elliot, don't." I hold up a hand.

"Fine. Don't tell me, but I know I'm right. I even told him you were smitten, and he said he was smitten with you."

"Elliot! You didn't! I could get fired."

"Girl, you think I'm going to tell on you? Nobody follows those crazy rules." He bats his hand at the air. "Do you know how many models I've found in the closet, and don't get me started on the makeup girls."

"No. Melanie and Victoria?"

"Yeah, they don't follow the rules so much," Elliot tsks with a conspiratorial grin.

"You're a terrible gossip. I don't want to know this. And now that you've told me all this, how will I know you'd keep a secret if I told you one?"

"I'll keep any secret you have if you let me go help that caterer finish cleaning up." He looks over my shoulder with glee.

I straighten my back and raise my voice. "Elliot, will you please finish cleaning up the catering? I need to check in with Alana and let her know how everything went today."

"Sure thing, boss." He salutes me, and I leave the studio so I can't incriminate myself and head to Alana's office.

❄

"Hey Morgan, I was just getting ready to come check on you. Are you guys done for the day?" Alana says in way of greeting me when I walk in.

"Yes. Everything went smoothly. Once Ty—Mr. Hudson loosened up, things went a lot faster."

"Oh great."

"Simon will have the proofs ready for us tomorrow."

"Okay, let's review them together. Make sure we don't need to bring Mr. Hudson back in. Then we'll find out when Tanya can come take a look."

"Sounds like a plan. What else do you need from me today?"

Alana looks at her watch and then back up. "Nothing. It's almost the end of the day, so why don't you leave early, and we'll regroup tomorrow. I have a list of new tasks and our next photo session to finalize before I leave. I'll go over that with you tomorrow."

"Great. Thank you. I really enjoyed working with the team today."

"And no one came looking for me, which means you ran a tight ship. Not all of the sessions will be this easy, but I'm glad you got to start off on the right foot. Have a good night." Alana dismisses me with a smile and a small wave, and I walk to my office to grab my bag.

I decide to let the car service drive me home. Although it's a short walk, the adrenaline of the day has officially worn off, and now I can't get home fast enough to fall into bed.

My phone rings as I'm shutting my apartment door and dropping the keys on the small table next to it.

"Hello."

"Hello, Ms. Pierce or can I finally call you Morgan again?" Ty says in greeting.

"Morgan is just fine," I say with a yawn.

"Good, I missed you."

"How could you miss me when we were together all day?" I ask, making my way to my bedroom to undress as we talk.

"I was with Ms. Pierce today. I missed Morgan."

"Oh, *I* see," I say, with a hint of sarcasm.

"Can I come over?"

"I would love you to, but I've got one foot in my pajamas already and I'm about to fall into bed."

"It's four-thirty!"

"I know. I had the car bring me home because I couldn't even put one foot in front of the other. As soon as Alana said I could leave early, my energy meter plummeted to empty."

"Got it. Well, for what it's worth, I think we made a good team today, and I wanted you to know I'm proud of you."

"Thank you, Ty, that's sweet." I let out an audible yawn.

"Get some rest, and I'll talk to you tomorrow. Sweet dreams."

"You too."

I end the call, put my phone on the charger, and collapse into bed. I'm pretty sure I'll be out in … three … two … one.

CHAPTER EIGHTEEN
Tyler

It's only one thirty in California and since my evening just opened up, I decide to call Ben.

"Hey man, how's it going?" I ask when he answers.

"Everything is running smoothly."

"Okay, good. Anything new?" I ask.

"How about five new clients. All celebrities. Today."

"Nice!"

"Did you put out a new ad I didn't see?" Ben asks.

"No, I think a little friend of ours named Tanya might be the reason."

"Really? How come?" he asks.

"Uh, well, let's just say I did her a big favor, and my guess is she's returning said favor."

"You're not going to let me in on this?"

"It's embarrassing."

"Just tell me," Ben insists.

"Fine. I agreed to be the brand ambassador for her new men's workout clothing line."

"Like a model?" Ben starts laughing.

"This is why I didn't want to tell you."

"Oh, no, this is too good," Ben barely gets out in between his guffaws. "Man, my stomach hurts now."

"Serves you right for laughing at me. Just doing a friend a favor. Now it's over, and I can get back to work. Any of those clients coming to New York?"

"As a matter of fact, I've got two headed your way. I'm sending you their bios and goals. One is prepping for an action role, so it should be a lot of fun."

"Yes!" I pump my fist. "Action movie workouts are my favorite," I say in agreement.

"Maybe I'll be working you out for an action movie one day, Mr. Model," Ben goads.

"Like I told Tanya, that's a no for me. She's lucky I agreed to the photo shoot."

"I've got a client coming in now so I gotta run. Talk to ya later, buddy."

"Thanks Ben. Talk soon."

After I hang up, I check my emails for the bios and then start planning the workouts. Before I know it, my stomach is growling, and I realize I haven't had dinner.

I grab my phone. "Bro, where you at?" I ask when Oliver answers.

"Ally's."

"Cool." I hang up and march over to Allison's and knock on her door.

"Hel-lo Ty-ler," Allison sings as she swings open the door.

"Hey, you guys eat dinner yet?" I ask, making my way into her living room to sit next to Oliver.

"Come on in. Make yourself at home," Allison says sarcastically, closing the door and joining us.

"Why aren't you at *your* girlfriend's house bothering her?" Oliver asks.

"One, she's not my girlfriend yet and two, she's asleep. We had a long day today, and she was exhausted, so I called Ben, did some work, and now I'm here bothering you two."

"I'm not sure I like how close we are anymore. Are you sure you aren't needed in California?" Oliver jokes.

"As a matter of fact, I just got two new celebrity clients coming here," I proudly announce.

"Celebrity?" Allison pipes up with excitement written all over her face.

"Yep!"

"Men or women?" she asks, standing in the middle of the room in shock.

"Both men and one is training for an action movie."

"Oh my God. Please say, it's Harry Hutchins." She starts to fan her face.

"Hey," Oliver blurts out.

"Oh stop. You'd act the same way if your beloved Scarlett was training next door," Allison sasses back.

"Oh busted." I laugh and Oliver gives me the stink eye. I quickly recover and continue, "I can't say. Client confidentiality." I keep a straight face revealing nothing.

"I hate you. That's so not fair," she says, finally taking a seat with a fake pout.

"So, anyway, you guys want to get some dinner?" I ask, changing the subject.

"Sure. We were going to order Chinese, you in?" Oliver says.

"Sounds great. I'll have steamed chicken with vegetables."

"I'll call in the order," Allison says and walks into the kitchen so Oliver and I can talk.

"So, how did it go today?"

"Great. I was a little nervous at first but then got the hang of it. That's why we got done early."

"Awesome. And I take it you kept yourself in check?"

I grimace.

"Dude!"

"What? So, I flirted a little. No one seemed to care. Morgan remained professional, but get this, her assistant walked me out and told me he could tell she was smitten with me." I laugh.

"He actually used the word smitten?" Oliver laughs along with me.

"Yep. So, I think it will be okay. And besides, we're done. I just had to do this gym shoot. Now Morgan can move onto bigger and better things, and I can go back to training, and we can continue on this road and see where it takes our relationship."

Allison returns and curls into Oliver's side. It makes me miss Morgan.

"What'd I miss?"

"Ty is head over heels in love with Morgan and wants to be a model," Oliver teases.

"He does not," Allison swats his arm.

"Okay, he doesn't want to be a model," Oliver corrects.

"But he's in love with Morgan?" Allison asks, turning her attention to me. I lean back.

"Both of you cut it out. You know Morgan and I agreed to just be open to whatever comes."

"And you know that I think that sounds like a perfect idea for you two," Allison agrees.

"You might think so, but I bet that they won't be able to keep their hands off each other until this is over," Oliver says to Allison.

"Did I hear the word bet?" I ask.

"You know you did." Oliver squints at me and leans forward with his arms resting on his legs.

"I'll take that bet," I return with the same determined look.

"Shouldn't Morgan have a say in this?" Allison interjects.

"She doesn't need one because I'm not going to lose," I say, puffing out my chest at Oliver.

"Uh, huh, we'll see," Oliver replies, sitting back.

"Look we're taking this slow and I'm not messing up her job for her, so you can quit acting cocky right now," I profess.

"Okay, that's fine." Oliver raises his hand in defeat. "But … if I win, you have to clean up Thanksgiving dinner," he adds with a smirk.

"Oh, you do not want to make that bet," I say, shaking my head.

"I think I just did," Oliver states, holding out his hand.

"I hate to see you lose this one. I'm sorry Allison, but you might not see Oliver for a few weeks. Mom is the best cook, but she literally uses every pot and pan when she cooks for the holidays," I explain and then shake Oliver's hand to confirm the bet. As we shake there's a knock at the door.

We spread the food out on the coffee table and spend the evening talking about Oliver's book, Allison's newest client from hell, and their never-ending guessing of who my new clients are. When exhaustion finally strikes, I excuse myself back to my apartment and fall into a deep sleep where I dream of losing the bet.

CHAPTER NINETEEN
Morgan

A LANA WASN'T KIDDING when she said she'd have a task list for me. It's been a whirlwind of activity and photo shoots since I saw Tyler last. Tanya has yet to review the photos due to some scheduling conflicts, so I guess it's for the best that I haven't seen Tyler so there's no temptation before his contracted work is officially completed.

I haven't even been able to have a decent conversation with Ally. Speak of the devil, her name appears on my phone screen.

"Hey, what's up?" I answer.

"Thanksgiving."

"What about it?"

"Ellen wants us to come to her house."

"Who's us?"

"All four of us. You, me, Oliver, and Tyler."

"Why wouldn't we do what we always do? Me with my mom and you with your crazy brothers and parents."

"I just found out that Mom and Dad are going on a cruise, so my brothers are going to their in-laws and I'm all alone. Ellen wouldn't hear of it, so I'm invited, and she invited you."

"I'd have to talk to my mom. I can't leave her alone."

"I know. And I know Ellen wouldn't mind adding another place at the table for her. Call Mom and let me know."

"All right. I'll call you back." Ally's been calling my mom, Mom, since they met and immediately bonded over the need to hug everyone they meet.

I quickly dial my mom's number. I might as well get this over with. She loves to cook and spoil me so I'm not sure how she'll take it. Plus, I may not have told her about Tyler yet.

"Hey, Mom," I say when she answers.

"Hi, Honey. What a surprise to hear from you in the middle of the day."

"Yeah, I just off the phone with Ally and her parents are going on a cruise for Thanksgiving and—"

"You want her to come here with you? That's terrific. I'd love to have her."

"Actually, she's been invited to her new boyfriend's house, and I was invited to go with them."

"Oh," Mom's voice breaks.

"No, no, it's not like that." I sigh. "Okay, here goes. I met her boyfriend's brother at the last bar hop and we're sorta kinda dating, so his mom invited all of us to go to her house and that includes you."

"You met a guy?" Mom's voice perks up.

"Yeah, but don't get too excited. It's all new and there's a whole thing with work that I'll fill you in on later."

"That's wonderful. I'm sure it will work out if you give it a chance."

"I'm trying."

"It's worth it."

"Is it? I'm surprised to hear you say that."

"I know it hasn't been easy since your father left but don't let that influence how you approach new relationships."

"Hasn't been easy? That's an understatement," I say, tersely.

"Morgan. Watch your tone."

"Fine. Fine. Look, I just called to see if you would be okay with going to a Thanksgiving dinner instead of making it."

"As long as I get to spend time with you, I'll do whatever makes you happy."

"Thanks Mom. I'll send you the details when I know what they are."

"Okay, love you, honey."

"Love you too."

I sigh and hold my head in my hands. My mom can

be a lot to deal with sometimes. I'm rubbing the stress from my temples when the intercom beeps.

Alana calls me into her office to go over more tasks, and I suddenly can't wait for the few days off we have for Thanksgiving. I'm exhausted. And I'm really looking forward to seeing Tyler. I didn't think this no-dating thing would be a big deal but seeing him in small doses is making me want him more. I'll call him tonight to coordinate this Thanksgiving situation.

❄

I PULL OUT my phone to call Tyler as I leave work and start to head home. "Hey," I greet when he answers.

"Hey, you getting off work?"

"Yeah. I'm walking home now," I tell him as I step into the flow of the foot traffic.

"Why don't you walk here?" he asks.

"I'd love that," I say quickly. "It's freezing and your place is closer." I turn toward his place.

"You just want me for a warm place?" he asks in a teasing tone.

"I want you for a warm body," I purr.

"Is that right?" he replies with a hint of salaciousness in his voice.

"Uh-huh." I blush.

"Well get over here." I pick up my pace.

"I'm walking as fast as I can. I'll be there in a few," I say before hanging up and taking off in a run.

I don't know what's come over me but the need to see and touch Tyler is strong, and I don't want to deny my feelings anymore.

Tyler flings open the door when I knock, and I jump into his arms.

"Well, that's a hello I can get behind," Tyler says, nuzzling his nose in my neck before putting me down. "Did you hear back from Tanya yet?" he asks, closing the door and taking my coat.

"No, I'm getting a little frustrated with the whole situation."

"I can tell." He smirks. "It usually doesn't affect your personal life like this though. Are you sure you don't want me to say anything now that it's dragging out?"

I sigh, a deep soul-searching sigh, and sit on a bar stool. My lady bits are dancing and chanting, "Tell them. Tell them," but I squeeze my legs together to drown them out.

"I don't know. I wanted to prove myself. Show them what I could do and not get preference because I was your girlfriend. But now my mind is a mess. I don't know what to call us because we've only been on a few dates and had sex. Everything feels backwards."

"Yeah, we did kinda do this backwards. Look, if you still want to keep it a secret it's fine with me, but there's nothing that says we can't do anything when we aren't working together, right?"

"Hmm, keep talking."

"No pressure at all, but if you say you're ready to go, I'm all in."

"Thanks, Tyler. I've never met anyone like you before. You are quickly getting through my typical defenses," I admit.

He smiles and places a gentle kiss on my lips. I'm about to return the kiss with one of my own when there's a knock at the door, and I jump back. Tyler growls and walks to the door.

"Hi guys," Ally says, walking in the door with Oliver in tow.

"What's up?" Ty asks.

"I saw that Morgan was here, and we wanted to know if you guys wanted to go to that multi-level arcade tonight," Ally says, coming to lean on the breakfast bar.

"How did you know I was here?"

"The tracker app. Remember when we put them on our phones?" Ally says, holding up her phone.

"Oh yeah," I admit, nodding my head.

"Thank you for your concern for my well-being when you didn't even remember you had the app," Ally huffs in mock disgust.

"Get over it. You have Oliver now," I tease.

"So, do you guys wanna go?" Ally asks, breaking

character and getting back to business.

"Sure. But I'd like to change first," I say.

"How about I walk you home so you can get changed and then we can meet up with you guys at the arcade in like an hour?" Ty addresses all of us and looks at his watch.

"Sounds like a plan. I'll text you the address," Oliver says and then he and Ally walk back to her apartment.

Tyler helps me back into my coat and locks up. When we get to the sidewalk, I wrap my arm through his.

"Oh, hey, I talked to Ally and my mom, so it looks like we're all going to your mom's for Thanksgiving," I start, trying to make conversation to keep my teeth from chattering.

"I was going to ask you about that. That's great. I'll let my mom know."

"Yeah, Ally called me earlier, and I called my mom to get it out of the way. I wasn't sure how she'd feel about it, but she was on board. Said she'd do whatever made me happy."

"And being with my family for Thanksgiving makes you happy?" Tyler asks.

"It does," I admit. "My mom is pretty emotional when it comes to holidays and sometimes it's hard to handle on my own, so hopefully this will make her happier too."

"I had no idea."

"You wouldn't because we haven't had the 'past' talk."

"I believe I asked you to tell me about yourself on our first date and you left out a few things."

"It was a first date. I didn't want to scare you off." I shrug as we climb the steps to my building.

"You'd be amazed at some of the first dates I've had. I'm not sure what scares me at this point." Tyler laughs.

We walk into my place, and I bump the small table by the door. Several travel brochures I collected for my dream board fall on the floor and Tyler picks them up.

"What are these?" he asks, putting them back in a neat pile on the table.

"Dreams," I tell him but don't elaborate. "You were saying you've had some winners?" I ask to bring the focus back to him.

"You could say that," Tyler admits, helping me out of my coat and then taking his off.

"Just leave them on the couch," I tell Tyler, addressing the coats. "Give me a few minutes to change."

Tyler sits on the couch, and I move to my room.

"You know, we'll probably end up with two meals because my mom loves to cook too," I shout from my room as I pick out a sweater and jeans to wear.

"Bring it. It's one day I don't worry about the calories," he calls back.

"Good. I don't think you'd have a choice if you did." I laugh as I pull the sweater over my head.

"I can't wait to meet your mom. Do you think she'll like me?" Tyler asks when I rejoin him in my living space.

"Truthfully, yes. She's ready for me to settle down." I slip on my sneakers that are lined up by the door.

"Is she going to ask when we're getting married?"

"I can't say she won't, but I did tell her that we're still trying to figure out what's going on here."

Tyler comes over to stand in front of me and grabs both my hands.

"Morgan, let's cut to the chase. I like you. I want to have a relationship with you. I don't want to date, see, or talk to anyone else. So, for me, that means I'm your boyfriend and you're my girlfriend if anyone asks. Until you're ready to jump in, you can call it whatever you want, but I'm just going to make it easy for myself." *Fortress hit ... seven?* That's it. The fortress walls have fallen. The door to my heart is exposed. It's still locked but there's a possibility that Tyler will finally be able to unlock it.

I lean up and kiss him on the lips. No one has ever told me they want me like this, and if Tyler Hudson wants to be my boyfriend, then screw it, I'm in.

"I'm in." He picks me up and spins me around.

"Good. Now, are you ready to go kick some butt at

the arcade?" he asks, putting me down and smacking my butt.

"Yes! Let's go!" I cheer.

We put our coats back on and march out the door.

CHAPTER TWENTY
Tyler

MORGAN CUDDLED INTO me when we got in the cab and laced her fingers through mine. I zoned out as we sped past the sights and absently stroked her fingers.

"I like that. It's very calming," Morgan whispers.

"What's calming?" I ask, bringing my focus back to her.

"What you're doing to my hand. I like it."

"Wow, I didn't realize. I'm glad it didn't bother you."

"It's nice." I pull her to my side and kiss the top of her head. "That's nice too," she admits, and I huff out a laugh.

It's like once we got over what to call our relationship, the annoying buzz of the unknown stopped and was replaced by a much calmer one. One filled with new-relationship tingles. One that says that holding her, touching her, kissing her is allowed.

"It sounds like you and Oliver are quite competitive. Are you going to win me a big prize tonight?" Morgan asks.

"The biggest. Yours will be bigger than whatever Oliver gets Allison," I boast.

"Good. I'm highly competitive myself, and I can't be dating a slouch."

"I can understand that, and you are definitely not dating a slouch."

"What's your game? Like what are you best at?" Morgan asks, waving her hand around.

"Hands down, Skee-Ball. What about you?"

"The ball drop if they have it. I'm pretty good at finding the pacing."

"That's a tough one for me. It's good we have different skills," I admit and pull her in for another kiss. "Let me know if I'm giving you too many kisses."

"I don't think that's possible. When I said I was in. I meant I was *all* in."

"All?" I say in question.

"All. As in nothing is off the table." She winks and there's a twitch in my pants.

"Then we better get in there and beat them and get back to my place," I say as we pull up to the curb outside the arcade.

"Have I mentioned that I like the way you think?" Morgan murmurs in my ear before I exit the cab. The cold air hits at the perfect time to cool my excited nerves. I help her out of the car, and we meet Allison and Oliver in the lobby.

"Let me guess, you're off to Skee-Ball," Oliver says as we approach.

"You know it. And Morgan is going to walk out with the biggest prize on the wall," I declare with confidence.

"I feel like there is a bet coming on," Oliver says with a gleam in his eye. "You're not ready to make another one, are you? I'd hate to see you lose twice." He rubs his hands together like an evil villain. Sometimes I worry that his books are rubbing off on him.

"More like I'd hate to see *you* lose twice," I quip.

"A hundred bucks. Most tickets wins. Loser buys dinner," Oliver states the terms and holds out his hand.

"Deal," I say and shake his hand.

"Deal."

We load a hundred dollars on each of our play cards and take off in different directions. Morgan and I run to our go-to games to start. When we start losing, we quickly switch up and run to the different games that give out tickets, looking for better options.

When we're out of credits we take our cards to the prize area and add them together. We have enough to get a decent-sized bear but not the biggest. We have a few credits left to buy some loose candy and eat it while we wait for Allison and Oliver to come back.

A few minutes later, Allison and Oliver are hooting and hollering as they make their way to the prize area.

"We won the jackpot at the ball drop and we both got a thousand on the big bass wheel," Oliver cheers ready to claim victory.

"Okay, okay smartass, let's see what you got all together," I say, pumping my arms for him to slow his roll.

When they add it up Oliver is shy a few points to win the same level bear that I got Morgan.

"Oh. Denied. Sorry your man wasn't up to the task," I say to Allison.

"Oh, he's always up for the task," she sasses.

"La, la, la, la," I shout, covering my ears. Everyone laughs while he picks out a smaller bear. Then we decide to hit the restaurant that is connected next door.

"Dinner's on me. Let's go," Oliver concedes, and we follow him out the door.

We order pizza, salads, and beer.

"I see you two aren't keeping your distance anymore," Oliver says after we order.

"For all intents and purposes, I officially declare that Morgan is my girlfriend. I will not cause her any grief at work, but we are no longer keeping our distance after hours," I decree to the whole table and anyone else listening.

"Wow, so looks like I won't have to do dish duty on Thanksgiving, sweet bro." Oliver pumps his fist in victory.

"I wouldn't say that. Not yet anyway," I say, trying to squash his expectations.

"Oh real-ly," he draws out. "We'll see. You forget I'm your twin. I know you and would be surprised if you had that level of restraint." Oliver rubs his chin.

"Dude, you've seen what I can do when prepping for a show, right? It's the same determination, and if I get to beat you again, it's worth it."

"What's all this about?" Morgan asks, looking between the three of us.

"Tyler and I have a bet going and the loser has to do Thanksgiving clean up," Oliver says, omitting what's really at stake.

Before we can take the conversation any further, the pizza and salads are delivered to our table, and we dig in. The conversation turns to Oliver's book, and I'm thankful I don't have to explain the bet to Morgan right now. Sometimes having a famous brother can be convenient.

After we finish eating, we all take a cab back to my and Allison's building.

"You still want to come up?" I ask Morgan after she pauses at the front steps and looks down the street toward her place.

She looks back up the stairs and nods. "Yes."

We say goodnight to Allison and Oliver in the hallway, and then I take her coat when we get inside my apartment.

"Would you like something to drink?" I ask.

"I'll take a water, thank you."

"Coming right up." I grab a bottle of water from the fridge and open it for her. "Do you want a glass?"

"No, the bottle is fine. Thank you for a great night. I had a good time, and I love my bear." She squeezes the bear and then sets it on the counter before taking a sip of water.

"You're welcome. It was a lot of fun. And we got a free dinner." I wink.

"So, what's the deal with the other bet?"

"Promise me you won't get mad," I say, coming to stand in front of her.

"Nope. I can't promise until I know what it is," she answers honestly.

"Okay, here goes," I start, holding my hands out in front of me as if that will keep her calm. "Oliver bet me we couldn't keep our hands off each other until the photo shoot was done. Loser has to clean up after my mom on Thanksgiving." Morgan stares at me and twists her lips in thought. I drop my hands to protect my privates in case she's ready to punch me, but then she speaks.

"Can I see your phone?"

"Sure. Why?" I ask, pulling it from my pocket and

handing it to her.

Morgan taps on the screen and holds it up for me to see. There is a text to Oliver that says: You win. Dishes are on me.

"What?" I gasp and look up at Morgan who has a wicked gleam in her eye.

She continues to hold the phone up so I can watch her hit send then she takes my hand and leads me to the bedroom.

As we're panting side by side, Morgan speaks first.

"How messy is your mom?"

"Very," I huff out.

"Worth it," Morgan proclaims. "But why didn't you tell me about it sooner?"

"I didn't think it would even be an option with the dating prohibition. I thought it would be an easy win."

"You forgot how hot you were. I tried. I tried hard, but every time you'd get into a new pose, I wondered what it would be like to take you right then and there," Morgan admits.

"I do have a gym in the other room if you want to try anything out. I'm happy to oblige."

"I'll keep that in mind." Morgan straddles me, and I couldn't care less how many dishes we have to do. To quote Morgan, it's "worth it".

CHAPTER TWENTY-ONE
Morgan

I'M DOODLING ON my iPad when Elliot comes into my office with a bag containing our lunches so we can eat at my desk and keep working.

"What's that?" he asks, setting out the containers.

"I'm working on some designs I'd like to show Tanya when this is all over," I explain, turning the device for him to see.

"Oh really, that would be amazing. You'd be a designer to the stars," Elliot says, waving his hand with a flourish. "Tanya, who are you wearing? Morgan Pierce? Isn't she fabulous? You look amazing." Elliot rattles off into rolled-up plasticware as if he's interviewing Tanya on the red carpet.

"That is the dream," I admit.

"You'll make it happen. I know you will."

"Thanks, El." He nods and takes his sandwich out of its container.

"So, are we finally going to talk about you and

Hunky Hudson?"

I whip my head around.

"Elliot, shh, I don't want anyone to know about us," I whisper, waving my hand to quiet him.

"Why not? The shoot is over. We're done. You can date whoever you want." He shrugs.

"It's technically not over until Tanya signs off, and she hasn't done that." I start to open my lunch container.

"You can't deny the heat between you two."

"Do you think everyone else could tell?" I ask in concern, my hand gripping the box so hard the Styrofoam squeaks under my hand.

"He was clearly flirting with you, but you kept it professional, so I don't think you'd get into any trouble even if someone said something to Alana. Plus, I'd totally vouch for you," Elliot says, slightly calming my nerves.

"Of course there's heat. There's always heat when it's new," I confess.

"And you totally got some last night, didn't you."

"How on earth can you tell?"

"The glow." I throw a potato chip at him and take a bite of my sandwich.

"You're too perceptive for your own good."

"It's a gift," he nods and takes another bite of his food.

"Well, keep your gift to yourself. I don't need everyone to know. Besides, why would I show my cards now when I don't even know if it will last. I mean, what happens when we're both working long hours and can't see each other? Or what happens when I get old and wrinkled? He's a bodybuilder for crying out loud. He could leave me for a newer model, literally."

"Girl. Stop. You need to caaalm down," he draws out, holding out his hand in a calming motion. "You are way too up in your head about this."

"I don't think I am. It's what happens. No one talks about what happens after Cinderella marries Prince Charming. Sure, they'd have staff, but she's got to run the household and help keep the people of the land happy." I gesture with my hand at the endless possibilities, and now Elliot is officially laughing at me.

"I'd like to think that Prince Charming puts her on the pedestal she deserves and treats her like the queen she will become, and he will ravish her for the rest of their days." Elliot sighs with a far-off look on his face.

"Fairy tales are baloney."

"Stop being so cynical and just let yourself go."

"Hmmph," I grumble, taking a chomp out of my sandwich.

"I'm assuming he's good in bed, given the glow?" he asks, taking a sip of water.

"Where are you going with this?"

"Have you ever been with anyone like him before?"

"No," I admit.

"Don't you think his body alone is a good enough reason to see where this goes?"

"Bodies come and go. It's what's inside that lasts and that's the part that that terrifies me." I can't believe I just admitted that out loud. I didn't think last night, I just went with what felt right, and now the doubt is creeping in.

"That's deep. You've clearly thought a lot about this, and you clearly want it to work since you're keeping it a secret from Alana. Stop worrying and let yourself go." Elliot starts to sing "Let It Go" from *Frozen*, and I throw my napkin at him.

"Finish your lunch so we can get back to work."

We eat in silence while he continues to hum the tune, and I give him the stink eye. Just as we're packing up our trash Alana pages me.

"Morgan, can you come to my office?" Alana chirps.

"Elliot is with me. Should he come too?"

"Yes, that's perfect. Thank you."

"We're being summoned by the boss. Let's go."

We stand and Elliot follows me to Alana's office.

"Please have a seat," Alana extends her hand to the chairs in front of her desk. "I've got great news. Tanya finally had a chance to look at those photos of Mr. Hudson, and she is over the moon. However, she's decided she wants to reshoot a few of the poses. We're going to have him come in Monday after the Thanksgiving break. Thankfully, we just need a few of him doing the curls, so we just need the wall with the exercise bands reset and then a few dumbbells. I believe we still have everything you need since we only returned the big equipment while we waited to hear back from her. Elliot, I've sent you the list of outfits to pull and a photo of the previous setup so you can prepare. Morgan, you'll be in charge of Mr. Hudson when he gets here. Make sure he's treated well, is comfortable, and poses correctly. I heard you had a good rapport with him last time. That is all."

Alana dismisses us with a few taps of her iPad, and we return to my office. I flop into my chair and lay my head on my desk. *Fan-flipping-tastic.*

"Good rapport. That's clever, and she didn't even realize what she said," Elliot says with a giggle, taking a seat in front of me.

"What am I going to do? They're going to know."

"They're not. Relax. Go enjoy your holiday. We've got this," he confides and leaves my office.

Relax my ass. No one understands me like Ally, so I call her on the way home from work.

"Tell me what to do," I say when she answers.

"I did," she says, knowing exactly what I'm talking about.

"I didn't like that option. Give me another one."

"I understand why you won't tell them at work, but why are you fighting this when Tyler already declared you his girlfriend?

"My mom and dad."

"You and Tyler are not them. Look, I didn't know your dad, but I know Oliver, and if Tyler is one-quarter the man Oliver is, he's not going to do what your dad did to your mom."

"I'm so scared to open my heart to him."

"Why?"

"Because he's the first person I've remotely thought about letting in. I'll admit he's breached the castle walls but the lock to the door is still in place."

"You know, for someone who hates fairy tales, you reference them a lot in your analogies, which clearly means you know it's right. We wouldn't even be having this conversation if it wasn't. You'd have moved on by now."

"What if it's because you're dating his brother and it seems romantic, but it's not real? What if it's just the great sex?"

"Morgan!!"

"Fine," I huff.

"You're literally giving me a headache. I can't make you fall in love with Tyler, but you clearly are because you've become a whiny pain in my butt since you met him and that's not the Morgan I know. So, Morgan-up and just let yourself go." *I swear if I hear the words "let it go" one more time ...*

"He has to come in for a reshoot," I say, changing the subject.

"So?"

"Elliot can tell we're having sex. Something about the glow. I'm worried everyone else will see it too."

"T.E.L.L. THEM!"

"If I lose this job, I'll lose my apartment. Are you going to let me live with you if I do?"

Bang. Bang. Bang.

"What's that sound? What are you doing?" I ask Ally.

"Literally banging my head on the wall. You're making me crazy. Which is why I state again that you are falling in love with this man!"

"Let me see how things go after he meets my mom. Then I'll decide."

"Fine. Can I go now? I need to find some Novocain to numb my brain after this conversation."

"Who's being the over-dramatic pain in the ass now?"

"Me. Gotta go. I'll see you tomorrow."

"Love you, Ally," I sing.

"Love you too," she sings back.

I'm already back at my apartment, so I strip out of my coat and fling myself across the bed.

CHAPTER TWENTY-TWO
Tyler

I'M CREATING NEW workout plans for next week when I get a call from Tanya.

"Tanya," I say in greeting.

"Tyyyler. How's my hunky trainer today?" She coos into the phone.

"Pretty good. How about you?"

"Great! I just got a look at your photos, and you are a natural!"

"Thanks. Glad I could help you out. I'm also glad it's done. Modeling life really isn't for me," I admit.

"About that …"

"Yes?" I say, wondering what she's about to rope me into now.

"I need you back in the studio on Monday."

"What? Why? You just said everything looked good."

"Most of them were. There are just a few really good poses that are a little blurry that I need you to redo."

"I've got clients."

"I know and I'm sorry, but I've got a casting call in California, and I need to wrap this up while I'm in town for the holiday," she rushes out.

"Fine. I'll get them rescheduled. What time do I need to be there?" I ask in defeat.

"Not until twelve."

"I'll be there."

"Yaaay." She claps in that way girls do when they get their way. "Thank you Ty-ler," she coos again.

"Will you be there?"

"No. Morgan will show you what to do. I know you'll be in good hands, right? Isn't that what you told me last time?" Her question sounds suggestive.

"I did," I say, purposefully not giving her any extra info.

"Come on Tyler, aren't you going to tell me what's going on with you two?"

"Nothing. She's a very nice woman who I wanted to do a good job for. Nothing more. You of all people should understand that."

"Wow, you really are being tight-lipped on this one. Must be serious."

"Tanya," I say in a warning tone.

"Fine. Fine. I won't push it. But she is cute, and I can totally understand why you'd be into her. She looks like a California girl, and I know that's your type."

"I hadn't really noticed," I divert.

"Ha! I'm not even going to believe that one. You don't have to share with me, but let's just say I can see you two being a good pair."

"Thanks for your observation. I will keep it in mind. Have a good weekend. I'll be there Monday at noon."

"Thank you so much! Talk soon." Tanya clicks off with a giggle, and I know I'm totally busted.

As soon as I hang up, Oliver calls.

"Hey bro, I need you. Be ready in half an hour."

"Why won't anyone let me do my job? I'm trying to start a business here. First Tanya, now you. What do you need?" I rant.

"Whoa. Don't take your frustrations out on me."

"What do you need?"

"Mom called and asked if we could move the furniture back into place in the basement so it looks nice for tomorrow."

"Can you give me an hour? I've got to move some things around and then I'll be ready."

"You got it. And don't think we're just going to gloss over that text message you sent last night."

"Oliver," I growl out his name in warning.

"Okay, okay man. Don't get bent. See you in an hour."

AN HOUR LATER, Oliver is at the curb waiting for me.

"Feeling better?" he asks.

"Yeah, I guess so. It's just a lot going on at once and everyone seems to need something from me, and I can't get traction. I can't be moving clients all over the place or they'll leave if they don't have a consistent schedule."

"I'm sorry. And I can relate. It's hard to be constantly interrupted and stay focused on your work. One time I got so distracted a knife created bullet holes in my victim." That gets me to laugh.

"Hopefully once we move all this stuff back Mom won't need us for a while."

"That would be nice, but don't get your hopes up. She can be a lot sometimes. It's like just when you think she's thriving on her own, along comes a flooded basement to throw everything off kilter."

"I'm really sorry you were all she had for so long, and I'm sorry for growling at you."

"I accept your apology, but I'm kinda surprised you're in a foul mood after the text I got last night."

I huff out a sigh.

"You like how I slipped that in?"

"No, but yes, we had a very good night. I really like her."

"Obviously. Is she okay with you calling her your girlfriend?"

"I think so. I just don't have the boyfriend label

confirmed."

"Do you think she's worth the trouble?"

"I'd like to think so."

"You just got here. Maybe it would be a good idea to date a few other people before you're hung up on one person."

"No. I told her there was no one else. I loved how carefree she seemed when we met. That was a nice change, but this new position has her flip-flopping like a pancake. Like she can't decide which side she wants to land on."

"That's one I haven't heard before. I hope she lands on your side." Oliver chuckles.

"Me too."

"You mentioned something about Tanya. What's up with that?"

"I need to go in for retakes and now I'm worried Morgan is going to freak out again and run away."

"Why don't you two talk over the weekend so you can assure her everything will be okay. It's just a few retakes. No big deal. You know what you're doing now, so I'm sure you'll be in and out."

"I'm sure you're right. You've always been the more level-headed of the two of us."

"I know," Oliver says as we pull into the driveway.

"Boys!" Mom sings as she opens the door and pulls us in for hugs.

"Hi Mom," we say in unison.

"Come on in, there isn't much to move, so it shouldn't take long. I've got to get the pies in the oven, so let me take you downstairs and tell you where to put it all."

"Wow, looks great, and it doesn't smell like mold," Oliver says, stepping off the last step.

"Tom fixed the plumbing and then I had a contractor paint and lay the new carpet."

"It does look nice Mom," I add.

"Thank you. I just need the couch to go here," she points to the long wall. "The two chairs to go here," she points to the side walls. "The coffee table will go in front of the couch, and this bookshelf can go on the wall at the bottom of the steps. And that's it."

"We're on it," Oliver says, and we start with the couch first.

"I'll be in the kitchen." She leaves us to work and walks up the steps.

"Why couldn't we have just done this tomorrow?" I ask.

"Because she wanted it done today and it's hard to say no."

"Got it," I say, knowing not to complain any further.

"You should have seen me lying on my back with water pouring down on me. That was not a fun day," Oliver huffs as we move the couch.

I start to laugh but quickly sober up when Oliver gives me a don't-you-dare look.

"I bet." We move the chairs in place and then the coffee table.

"I can laugh now that everything worked out and Ally understood why I couldn't call her. That was an utter mess for a while."

"I know. I'm glad it worked out too. You make a good couple."

"Thanks."

Once we put the bookshelf in place, we meet up with Mom in the kitchen.

"All done. Do you need anything else?" I ask.

"No, that was a big help. I want everything to look nice with the girls coming tomorrow. They may just be my future daughters-in-law."

"Ma," I start.

"Don't sass me boy. I can dream. And no, I won't embarrass either of you tomorrow. Now come give me a kiss and get out of here."

We kiss her at the same time on opposite cheeks and she giggles because we used to do it as kids.

"See you tomorrow, Mom," Oliver says as we walk out the door.

"Bye boys," Mom calls.

"Bye, love you," I call back.

Oliver and I get in the car and head back to the city.

He drops me off in front of my building.

"See ya tomorrow," I say, hopping out.

"I'll pick you guys up at eleven," he says.

"I'll be ready. Thanks."

"Did you see the pile of dishes already in the sink?" Oliver taunts, and I hang my head. "See ya." He lets out a maniacal laugh, and I slam the door before he pulls away from the curb.

CHAPTER TWENTY-THREE
Morgan

TYLER AND I coordinated with our mothers and now, Ally, Oliver, Ty, my mom, and I are standing at Ellen's front door. Ellen welcomes us with open arms and shows us to the kitchen. My mom follows with a full-size cooler in tow. I told Tyler there would be two meals today. I may have preemptively started looking up turkey leftover recipes for this very reason.

"Ellen, this is my mom Maggie," I introduce. Ellen immediately pulls my mom in for a hug.

"So nice to meet you. I'm glad you could come, and thank you for bringing so much food," Ellen says without the slightest bit of sarcasm.

"It's nice to meet you too. I've heard so much about all of you. Thank you for having us," Mom replies.

"Boys, get your drinks and take care of the girls while Maggie and I get the food ready," Ellen instructs.

"Yes ma'am," they say in unison.

Oliver and Ty take us into the den where there is a

bar with a drink station all set up and ready for us.

"Wow, you weren't kidding when you said your mom goes all out," I say to Tyler.

"She really does," Oliver agrees.

"Should we go help them?" Ally asks.

"No!" Ty and Oliver say in unison again. *Totally must be a twin thing.*

"You do not want to go in there. She has Maggie, that's enough. She doesn't like a lot of people in the kitchen when she's cooking. That's why we're in here," Oliver explains.

"Got it," Ally says, and we all sit on the matching loveseats in pairs.

"I'm so glad we got out of there before the parade ended. Thanksgiving travel is the worst when you're in the city."

"Yeah, we lucked out."

We hear laughter coming from the kitchen. I'm so thankful they are getting along. It would be nice if my mom had a new friend in Ellen. I think she would help her liven up a little.

We decide to play a game and pick *The Game of Life* from the stack under the coffee table. I become a teacher, Tyler is a doctor, Ally gets student, and Oliver is a lawyer. We laugh and tease each other until we're called to dinner.

The table is set with china on a fall-themed tablecloth. The plates have a dark green, marbled strip around the edge, and are trimmed in gold. The crystal drinking goblets have a matching gold rim. Everything is beautiful, and the matching candles complete the look.

"Everything looks terrific, Ellen. Thank you again for having us," Mom says, sincerely. I watch for glistening eyes and threatening tears, but all I see is joy. That is something I am most thankful for.

"You guys didn't tell me that Morgan didn't grow up too far from here. Maggie and I are practically neighbors," Ellen speaks up.

"Oh, yeah, I didn't realize where exactly you lived," I admit.

"Well, now that I have my new friend Maggie, we'll have to get together for coffee."

"I'd like that," Mom agrees.

"Can you believe all the kids are so close now? You and I can take the train into the city together to visit," Ellen continues.

"You will give us fair warning before you come, right?" Oliver asks with unease.

"Yes, Mr. Bigshot, we will respect your time," Ellen swats at him, and I laugh under my breath because I don't think his writing time was what he was worried about.

We continue the friendly and jovial banter all through dinner. When our mothers have made sure we are all stuffed to the gills, they allow us to leave the table.

"I'm told you and Morgan lost some bet, and I am relieved of clean-up duty?" Ellen questions Tyler.

"Yes, that's correct. We'll be in the kitchen until next Thanksgiving," Tyler teases.

"Oh you, stop it." Ellen smacks his shoulder. "I'll put the coffee on and then we can sit in the den until we serve dessert," Ellen tells my mom.

"Didn't you just have a renovation done in the basement?" Mom asks.

"I did. Come see." Ellen leads her down the steps, and Tyler and I get started on the dishes.

"Let's do all the china first. That way the pans can soak a bit longer."

"It's a plan."

Tyler washes and I dry, neatly stacking the plates on the dining room table for Ellen to put away.

After a few neck nuzzles, butt squeezes, and kisses, we finally finish and join everyone back in the den. I fall back on the couch, trying to give my stomach room to breathe. I should have brought my stretchy pants. Rookie mistake.

Ellen smacks her thighs and stands, offering us a choice of apple, pumpkin, or pecan pie. We all groan but can't pass up the offer and put in our orders. I help serve the coffee, and we eat in the den where it's more comfortable.

When we're finished, Ty and I wash the last few dishes while Ellen packs up the leftovers.

"This has just been a lovely day. Thank you, Ellen," Mom says, patting her stomach. "I can't wait for us to get together again." She picks up the handle of the cooler and pulls it to the door as we get our coats on. I think she may be leaving with as much food as she came with.

"You're welcome. It's so nice to have a full house. Please come any time." Ellen gives us each a hug before we pile into Oliver's car.

When we drop my mom back at her house, she gives me my share of the leftovers and a hug.

"Thank you, honey. That was just what I needed. And I totally approve of Tyler. I see the way he makes sure you're taken care of before he helps himself. That's something special."

"Thanks Mom. I'll keep that in mind. I'm glad you had a good time. I'll see you soon, okay?"

We hug one more time, and I hop back into the car.

"So, she said she liked me?" Tyler nudges my arm.

"She did."

"Did I hear the word "special" mentioned?

"Maybe?"

"She totally did." Tyler laughs. "For the record, she seems very nice and funny. She had me cracking up a few times with stories from her ladies' group." I laugh along with him.

"I'm glad you liked her. It makes me feel good to know you'll get along with each other." I can't sit up straight anymore and slouch down in the seat with a moan. "I don't think I've eaten that much food ever."

"It was all so good. Your mom's sweet potatoes totally rocked with the melted marshmallow on top," Oliver says to me.

"Yeah, that's her signature dish. I love them. I'm going to keep all the leftovers in Tyler's fridge, and we can all share from there," I say to the group.

"Sounds good to me. I'll be over for pie in the morning with coffee so make sure you two are decent," Ally chimes in with a giggle.

"Believe it or not, gym equipment sex isn't as cool as you think it would be, so all naked time stays in the bedroom," I reply.

"I seriously need to get the gym out of my apartment. Maybe I can finally look for a place once all this modeling stuff is done," Tyler says.

"Speaking of, when is that over?" Ally asks.

"Monday! Tanya finally looked over the original photos and just wants a few re-done and then we're free and clear," I exclaim.

"Whew, what a relief," Ally returns.

"Stop being dramatic," I sass back.

"Me? Who just called me yesterday in hysterics?"

"I would not call them hysterics, so please just drop

it," I say with warning in my voice.

"What happened yesterday?" Tyler asks. I glare at the back of Ally's head.

"Nothing. I was just nervous about the reshoot. Ally is blowing it out of proportion," I explain with a little fib.

"I'm sure everything will be fine," Tyler assures, pulling me into his side.

"Thank you." I nod, and then lay my head on his shoulder. Before I know it, I'm being nudged awake because Oliver just pulled up to Tyler and Ally's building.

"I assumed you'd stay the night with me," Tyler says, holding the door open and giving me his hand to help me out of the car.

"You assumed correctly." I yawn and thank Oliver for driving then follow Ally and Tyler up the stairs while Oliver parks the car.

"See you guys tomorrow?" Ally asks, before going into her apartment.

"Of course! You know what day it is," I confirm.

"Christmas movie day!" Ally and I shout in unison.

"What's going on?" Tyler asks.

"It's Black Friday. Every year, Ally and I sit on the couch, watch our favorite Christmas movies, and order Christmas presents online. The deals still apply, and we get to stay in our jammies and away from the crowds. It's also leftovers day, so we don't even worry about food," I explain.

"Does Oliver know about this?"

"About what?" Oliver asks, coming to a stop at the top of the stairs.

"Black Friday Christmas movie day," Tyler says.

"Yeah, Ally mentioned it. You want to check out the deals and run around the city with me while they do that?" Oliver asks Ty.

"I could use the exercise after today's caloric intake."

"Okay, great. Be ready by seven."

"And I'll see you at nine," I say to Ally.

We all hug and go into our respective apartments. I could get used to living here.

"Hang your coat on the hook, and I'll find you something to change into," Tyler states after he locks the door.

"Do you have a sweatshirt?"

"Sure do. Follow me."

I follow Tyler and we get changed in his bedroom. He grabs us some drinks, and we get situated on his bed to watch a movie.

"Before we start, can I ask why you say you're all in one minute and then pushing me away the next?" he asks.

"You're the first person I've ever worried about losing," I blurt out and clap my hand over my mouth in shock. *Stupid Ally, making me admit my feelings.*

Tyler gently removes my hand and replaces it with his lips.

"Thank you for being honest with me. I hope that you'll stay the rest of the weekend and let me show you how confident I am that you don't have to worry," he whispers over my mouth, and I pull him flush with my body.

We continue to make out until we're out of breath. I sit up and take a drink of water.

"Thank you for being patient with me. The job. You. It's all new to me, and I truly don't want to mess either one up."

"I can safely say that if you stay in my bed, you will not mess anything up with me." Tyler winks, and I smack his arm.

"That's one thing I know I'm good at. Admitting my feelings, not so good."

"You just took a big step in the right direction, and I appreciate it. I've dated women who've orchestrated our whole relationship down to what I should wear to which outing. So I need you to tell me when something's wrong, and it doesn't hurt to tell me when I'm doing something right." He kisses me.

"You definitely know what you're doing right," I say, kissing him back. "But I promise to be more forthcoming."

"That's all I ask. You ready to put the movie on?"

"Yes."

Tyler puts on *Miracle on 34th Street*. I curl into his shoulder and fall asleep before the drunk Santa finishes singing "Jingle Bells."

❄

TYLER AND OLIVER surprise us with breakfast set out on Ally's kitchen island when I arrive to watch our Christmas movie marathon.

"This was so nice of them," I coo.

"See? What did I tell you about Oliver? Tyler is just like him."

"You don't need to lecture me. I told Tyler last night that I was being weird because I was afraid of losing him. I promised to work on my communication skills."

"Well, hello, Morgan Pierce. I don't want to sound condescending, but I'm proud of you."

"I'm proud of me too. Now, let's take this food into your living room and get started."

Ally and I watch *Holiday in Handcuffs*, *Snowglobe*, and *The Most Wonderful Time of the Year* before Oliver and Ty return with lunch.

"You guys are spoiling us, and I love it," Ally cheers when they spread out the takeout containers on the coffee table.

"You know I'll spoil you anytime," Oliver returns.

Tyler leans over to me and whispers in my ear. "When I said I wanted open communication, it doesn't have to be this mushy."

"Whew, I was worried it would be a twin thing," I say, fake wiping my brow. He laughs.

"Definitely not."

"You guys, stop picking on us," Ally says with a fake pout.

"Hey, we're working on our own thing over here. This doesn't concern you," Tyler retorts.

"Fine. Fine. Maybe Oliver and I should kick you out then," she fake huffs.

"You mean, I can take my girlfriend and leave? Sweet." Tyler exclaims. Before Ally can answer, he jumps up and grabs me. "See ya later, losers." Tyler throws me over his shoulder and runs out of Ally's apartment.

I laugh all the way back to his apartment and when he plops me on his bed, let's just say, we don't see Ally or Oliver the rest of the weekend.

CHAPTER TWENTY-FOUR
Tyler

AFTER ONE OF the best weekends of my life, I hop out of bed early to get in a good workout before I leave for the reshoots. I must admit, the Monday after a holiday isn't the best time for this, but at least I won't be shirtless.

As I'm finishing up, Morgan walks out of my bedroom.

"Good morning," I say, giving her a peck on the lips.

"Good morning."

"Are you ready to go back to work today?" I ask, fixing a shake while Morgan pours herself some coffee.

"Not in the slightest," she admits, taking the first sip.

"At least I'll be there."

"I know. That's a pro and a con. Pro because you're there. Con because I have to keep my hands off you and after this weekend it won't be that easy.

"I promise to be on my best behavior," I pledge.

"Thank you. Now I better get dressed and get to

work." She leans up to give me a kiss. "And before you ask, no you can't walk me to work. I'll meet you there, Mr. Hudson."

"Yes ma'am."

I bundle Morgan into her coat and tuck her scarf around her neck before walking her down to the front door. We kiss and I watch her until she rounds the corner and is out of sight.

I quickly run back up the stairs to get ready. When I step back out onto the curb, the new December chill goes right through me. I hail a cab and am thankful for the warm heat blasting out of the vent. When we pull up to the front of Smyth Advertising, I take a deep breath to steady my nerves. I know what I'm doing now. I'll get in, take a few shots, and get out. I jog up the steps to the front door then walk straight to the front desk. A petite girl with jet-black hair and pale skin greets me with a smile.

"How can I help you, sir?"

"I'm Tyler Hudson. I'm here to see Morgan Pierce."

"Let me page her for you." She lets Morgan know I'm here and then smiles back at me. "She'll be right out to get you."

"Mr. Hudson. Good to see you again. Follow me," Morgan says as if I haven't ravished every inch of her body. She's wearing a blue top that makes her eyes pop and reminds me of the ocean. I can't look away.

"Ms. Pierce. Likewise," I return, keeping direct eye contact.

She fiddles with the hem of her top and turns for me to follow her down the long corridor to the studio.

"Elliot has your outfits ready. There will only be three changes today and just a few quick photos in each. Shouldn't take too long. Then you can be on your way." Morgan speaks in a clipped professional tone, revealing nothing. I cover my mouth to keep from laughing because I know what she's doing. We may have practiced how she'd keep her composure when she saw me over the weekend. We also may have practiced what she'd do if she didn't keep her composure, and that was a lot more fun.

When we enter the studio, the same group is there waiting to get me ready. I say hello to everyone and walk to the dressing room. Once I'm dressed and Melanie and Victoria are done with me, I walk into the makeshift gym.

"Please pose me as you wish, Ms. Pierce," I say, standing with my feet apart and my arms to my side as if I'm her puppet.

"Thank you for being agreeable, Mr. Hudson. We're just going to need a few upward rows to show off the muscles in your back."

I quietly do what's instructed. Simon circles me, then once he has the shots he needs, he lets me know I can go change.

"In this outfit, we're going to need a few shots on the chin-up bar," Morgan instructs. I nod and grab the bar. Once again, Simon zooms in and out and we're done.

"Final outfit will be a few of you in a seated position doing a stretch with the bands. Like this," Morgan sits and stretches out her leg and then wraps the band at the balls of her feet and pushes out."

"Got it." I sit and do as instructed. Once Simon is happy with his shots, I'm free to go.

When I come out of the changing room, the studio is empty except for Elliot, who's impatiently tapping his foot.

"What's up, Elliot?" I come to a stop in front of him and cross my arms.

"I'd like to know what was going on in here."

"Nothing. I came in, did my job, and got out." I shrug.

"Exactly. Why was I not seeing any flirting?" He whines.

"Because she asked me not to. I didn't want her to get fired."

"I don't want her to either. I could never do what she does. Anyway, now that the reshoot is done there's nothing to worry about. Can I be in the wedding?" I laugh.

"I think you're getting a little ahead of yourself there,

Elliot, but ultimately the wedding plans would be her decision."

"I just love watching couples fall in love," he gushes.

"I'm glad we could entertain you. But I admit, I'm glad this is all finally over."

"I'll miss you. Come on, I'll walk you out." Elliot pats my arm to guide me out of the door, and I follow him to the lobby.

Just as we're saying our goodbyes at the front desk, Tanya walks in the front door.

"Oh, this is terrific timing." She claps her hands in excitement.

"Tanya, I thought you weren't going to be here," I say in surprise.

"I wasn't supposed to, but then I got the best news! Come on, we need to talk to Alana!" she screams, dragging me by the wrist with Elliot in tow.

CHAPTER TWENTY-FIVE
Morgan

I'M IN ALANA'S office waiting for Simon to pull up the latest photos on his laptop. He's turning it to face us when the commotion of Tanya LeBoux waltzing into the office with an air of grandeur startles us. Tyler and Elliot follow behind as if footmen following a princess against their will. Ty is grimacing and Elliot is fiddling with his collar, his telltale sign he's nervous.

"Alana! I'm sorry to barge in like this, but I was too excited and had to come see you right away."

Alana stands and gives me a look that tells me to get up. I quickly stand and offer Tanya my chair.

"Thank you, Morgan," Tanya says and takes a seat.

"So, what's this news you're so excited about?" Alana asks, eyeing Tyler and Elliot before returning her eyes to Tanya and taking a seat in her desk chair."

"A snowstorm is going to hit Vermont this weekend!" Tanya claps.

"Could you give us a little more information," Alana

encourages. Tanya swivels in her chair left then right to make sure we're all listening.

"My designer just finished the men's outdoor line for my workout wear, and I'd like to use my family's cabin in Vermont for the photo shoot. With the snow coming we could get some great shots with real snow. What do you think?"

Tyler groans.

Elliot gasps.

Simon smirks.

And I'm trying to keep my jaw from hitting the floor.

"I'd have to make sure my team was available," Alana states calmly.

"I know it's last minute, but we can use my private jet, so we won't need to book flights," Tanya adds.

"Okay," Alana starts, smoothing out the papers on her desk. "Mr. Hudson, Elliot, Simon, can you all make it?"

Tanya gives Tyler puppy-dog eyes, and he relents. Elliot agrees, hopping on his toes in glee. Simon checks his phone and confirms. No one asks me, but who am I kidding, I'd never say no.

"Great. That makes my life easier. Thank you everyone. Mr. Hudson I'll need you to sign a new contract with Smyth Advertising. If you have a few minutes to wait, I'll make the necessary changes to the one you already signed and have Morgan go over it with you. Morgan, why don't you take Mr. Hudson to your office to wait, I'll get that over to you. Simon let's show Tanya the new photos and then you can go work your magic while Tanya and I go over the specs for this new outerwear collection. Elliot, standby. We'll get you a task list as soon as possible," Alana directs, commanding the room. We disperse. Tyler follows me back to my office, and I shut the door.

"Lord have mercy. When will this end? Why do you have to be so handsome?" I ask, shaking my fist after closing the door to my office.

"You're the one who told me to let loose and relax. Now look what you did?" Tyler banters back.

"And now you have another contract coming, which means I have to continue to keep up appearances until this shoot is over!" I practically shout in exasperation, but quickly quiet my voice. "What are we going to do?"

"If memory serves correctly, this only applies to working hours." He winks.

I nod with my whole body. "True. Very true. But I thought I only needed to get through a few more hours, not a whole weekend.

"We'll be fine. We can do this."

"We can?"

"Absolutely. I have complete faith in us," Tyler says. I want to run and hug him but pace the floor instead.

"Why don't we sit and wait for the contract," Ty suggests calmly.

"Good idea. Have a seat." I motion to the chairs in front of my desk.

Ty sits and starts looking around the room. "This is a nice office. I'm happy for you and don't want to cause you extra stress. I'll do what I did today. I'll get in and get out."

"Thank you. But now I'm starting to worry about myself more." I bite my thumbnail.

A new email notification pings on my computer and I open the document.

"Looks like it's all the same with the dates changed."

"And you still don't want me to talk to Tanya?"

"Correct."

"But it's only at the office, right?"

"Right," I affirm.

"Where do I sign?"

I send the doc to my iPad for him to sign and then forward it to Alana.

"I'll call you with the details when I have them."

With that, he nods and leaves my office.

***

IT'S BEEN A week, scrambling to get everything and everyone in place for the Vermont shoot, and I need to call Tyler to give him the details.

"Hello Mr. Hudson, it's Morgan Pierce from Smyth Advertising," I speak into the phone when he answers.

"Hello, Ms. Pierce. It's good to hear from you. I take it you have some news for me?"

"As a matter of fact, I do. We will need you to come to the office by seven a.m. Friday to take Tanya's private jet to Vermont."

"Will you be coming with us? To make sure I get in the correct positions?" He purrs into my ear. I'm so glad I don't have him on speakerphone.

"Actually, I will be going up on Thursday to prep the location."

"Alone?"

"Yes."

"I don't think that's very safe. Why isn't Elliot going with you?"

"He needs to stay here to receive the clothing from the courier and make sure the items are correct," I answer in my professional tone.

"I see. Well, as your boyfriend, I'd prefer it if I went with you. I'll speak to Tanya."

"What did you just say?" I ask, aghast.

"I'll speak with Tanya," he repeats.

"No. Before that."

"I'd prefer to go with you?"

"Before that," I say.

"Boyfriend?"

"Yes, that's the word I wasn't sure I heard correctly."

"You know how I feel," he says.

"I do, but it's the first time you've used it in a sentence."

"I see. So, what I'm hearing is that you're okay with me, but are worried about putting a label on it."

"Yes." I close my eyes at my admission.

"Don't be." My heart is beating out of my chest from the anxiety of this whole situation. *Why can't I just accept the label?*

"You don't understand, and I can't get into this with you right now."

"Fine, but I'm still coming with you for safety. I'll tell Tanya I have to be in place early to do online workouts with my clients on Friday."

"Okay. Thank you."

"You're welcome."

"Don't worry about a thing, I've got you g—Sorry, I won't say the word," he assures me in a calm voice, and my heart rate starts to return to normal.

"I've got to get back to my task list. Thank you. The car is picking me up at six a.m. Thursday morning. You can come to my place."

"I'll be there Wednesday night with bells on."

I disconnect without further objection and call the next person on my list.

CHAPTER TWENTY-SIX
Tyler

THE COMPANY CAR drops Morgan and me off in front of an A-frame ski lodge. Apparently, it's considered a single-family "cabin" by Tanya and her family. I take our bags from the driver and follow Morgan to the front door. She unlocks it and we enter this massive foyer with an antler chandelier hanging in the middle, set to a warm glow. The rest of the house is illuminated by sunlight streaming in the large windows. I've watched the weather reports and I know the storm is coming, but the bright blue sky gives me doubts.

"Should we look at the bedrooms first? Pick the best ones?" Morgan asks.

"Good idea. Let's go."

She runs up the double-wide staircase ahead of me and I follow with our suitcases. I appreciate that Morgan travels light.

After scoping out the eight bedrooms Morgan and I choose the two that are connected by a bathroom. I convinced her that it would make it easy for me to sneak in and out of her bed without being caught. Carefree Morgan has returned and agreed to the sleeping arrangements.

We remove our coats, hats, and gloves and go in search of the thermostat. We find it along the hallway to the kitchen and turn it up to a temperature that is tolerable before continuing our self-guided tour. We find that the kitchen is completely stocked with more food than we could imagine and decide to make some sandwiches.

"There's a pretty healthy selection here, but I'm glad I'm modeling outdoor clothing this time," I say, savoring the taste of the bread.

"Good point." She takes a bite of her sandwich and moans. "This is good. I was so hungry."

"Keep that up and you'll be lucky if I let you finish your lunch." She giggles. "I like that sound. I think I need to find a way to make you do that more often." She giggles again.

"Stop. Once I get the giggles I can't stop. We need to behave," she says.

"I promise I'll be good this weekend," I say, holding up my hand as if making a solemn vow.

"Thank you. We're almost done and then we'll be free to be whatever we want to be," Morgan states with a huge smile on her face.

"I volunteer as Morgan's boy toy," I say with a laugh.

"Is that all?" She feigns shock.

"Hey, you're the one who said she didn't want to put a label on it, so I'm all for having fun. For now." I wink. "So, tell me, what do we need to do first?" I ask, getting us off the topic of sex and onto the reason we're here.

"I need to bring up the list of poses. I know she wants ones by the fireplace to look like you're at a ski lodge. Hot cocoa, cozy setting, the works," she starts. "Then, I'll have to look at the rest. I think there was something about drinks at a bar. Did you see one?"

"No, but I bet there's a study or billiard room here somewhere that would work. By the way, shouldn't I have some ski bunnies with me? This is a men's and women's line."

"Their outfits aren't ready yet. We'll have to do those separately."

"Do I have to come back for that?" I grimace.

"As of right now, Tanya said she wanted to respect your time and asked if we could do some creative editing with the photos. That's on Simon. But don't rule it out."

"If they need me to come back, I'm telling Tanya about us. I don't want to hide this anymore. It's too stressful, and it's not fair to us."

"You're right."

"What did you just say?"

"I said, you're right. Don't make me regret it."

"I would never. Come here, girlfriend." I pull her in for a kiss.

"Say it again," Morgan whispers.

"Girlfriend," I repeat. She leans in and kisses me back.

"I'm going to let that sink in while we clean up, then we'll get started." We throw our trash away and wipe down the tables, and then Morgan grabs her iPad.

❄

ONCE WE'VE GONE through all the rooms and poses—yes, there is in fact a billiard room with a fully stocked bar—we collapse on the couch in front of the big stone fireplace.

"Do you want me to start us a fire?" I ask.

"Maybe later. We still have more work to do."

"Really?" I pout.

"Yeah, apparently there's a cute town square with lights that we need to check out. Tanya said she's going for ski-lodge elegance but wouldn't rule out a cute small-town vibe for some of the online accounts. To show that it can be for anyone who enjoys the outdoors."

"When do you want to head out?"

"Just give me a few minutes and then we'll go," Morgan says, closing her eyes and leaning her head on my shoulder.

When she starts softly snoring, I gently lay her down and cover her with the blanket hanging over the back of the couch, letting her get some rest. I grab some firewood from the side porch near the great room to build a fire. Once the fire is finally roaring, I pick out a blanket off the pile next to the mantel and lay down on the opposite couch.

A few hours later, I shiver and wake to find the fire has died down and Morgan is stirring.

"Did you have a nice nap?" I ask, as I rise to a sitting position.

"Yes, I feel great." She stands and stretches. "I'm kinda hungry. Want to make something?"

"I was thinking that we could check out that town square where Tanya wants us to take pictures. Maybe there's a little café where we can get some food and then walk around."

"That sounds great. Let's get some warmer clothes on and go."

We fold the blankets and I follow her upstairs to get changed.

When we step out onto the porch, snowflakes start to fall from the sky.

"Uh, this is starting a little earlier than they thought," Morgan says with a worried tone.

"It's just a few flakes. I'm sure it will be fine. Come on. I'm starving." I grab her hand and we walk the few blocks to the town square.

CHAPTER TWENTY-SEVEN
Morgan

WHEN TYLER AND I get to the square, it's like we stepped into a snow globe. There is a gazebo right in the middle with twinkle lights neatly hung around the edges of the roof, and Christmas music is playing from hidden speakers. The streetlamps look like old-fashioned oil lamps and are decorated with wreathes and garland and finished off with big red bows. The snow is softly falling, and I know when it stops, the photos of Tyler in the new line will be incredible. I know Simon will capture that small-town vibe that Tanya wants to show: You don't have to work out to enjoy her outerwear collection.

A brightly lit marquee beckons us and as we get closer, we see that it's for a small diner, and the smells coming from the exhaust make my mouth water.

"Wow. That smells amazing. My stomach is literally growling right now," I say.

"Mine too," Tyler admits, holding the door open for

me.

"Seat yourself," a plump brunette shouts from behind the counter when we enter.

We pick a booth along the front window so we can watch the activity on the main street.

"Now I know why they film Hallmark movies in these towns. It's beautiful here," I sigh.

"It is," Tyler affirms. "I thought you didn't like mushy romance movies. How do you know where they're filmed?"

"Busted. I looked it up when Ally started making me watch the Christmas ones."

"So, you admit to liking those sappy movies?

"Maybe?" I shrug noncommittally. "All those fairy tales of true love … I used to hate them because they're not real life. And the movies about moving to a small town to slow down so that you can see love before it passes you by are also not real. But seeing it in person makes it all seem possible." I gesture with my hand at the view out the window.

"I agree. You do have to slow down and let love in," Tyler says, and it looks like he wants to say more but he stops.

I grab his hand. "I hear you. And sitting here in this magical place, I don't just want you to be a boy toy," I admit.

"No? Then are you going to tell me what you want

me to be? He asks with a mischievous tone in his voice.

"I think you know."

"I think I need to hear you say it," he says, making my heart race and causing it to hit up against the locked door.

I take a deep breath. "Boy ... friend," I concede, the word coming out in two parts.

"Thank you." He squeezes my hand, and my heart is jumping up and down in glee. *Heart, you're winning.*

We take a minute to look at the menus and once we've decided, I move on from the mushy talk.

"Oh, I may have drawn up some designs for Tanya."

"You did? That's great. You should show them to her."

"You haven't even seen them. They might not be good enough."

"You don't know until you show them to her." He gives me a serious look.

"Maybe I will once this is over."

"I think you should remove the word, maybe, from that sentence.

"*Maybe* I will," I say with a satisfied smile on my face.

"What can I get you?" the waitress asks, approaching the table.

"I'll have an open-faced turkey sandwich and an iced tea," I order.

"I'll have a burger, no bun, and a side salad with a water," Ty adds.

"Got it. Be right back with those drinks." The waitress toddles off and we watch the snow fall.

"Do you think this is the beginning of the snowstorm Tanya was talking about?" I ask.

"Let me see." Tyler takes out his phone and brings up the weather app. "Looks like this is just a few flurries from the outer band and there should be a break before the big snow hits."

"Okay, good," I say, feeling relieved.

The waitress brings our drinks and lets us know the food will be out shortly.

"Looks like there are a few shops open that we can check out after we're done," I say, looking up and down the street.

"Maybe we can get a few more Christmas presents," Tyler suggests.

"It would be nice to find a few more things. Ally and I did a pretty good job online, but I love looking at all the small shops for rare finds."

Our waitress brings our meals and we dive in. The food is delicious and perfect for a cold snowy night. I can't hide the smile on my face, and I don't want to. I'm so glad I get this extra night with Tyler.

When we finish our food, we pay the bill and then tour the local shops.

We flow in and out of the quaint shops. From jewelry to housewares and homemade items. When we walk into a store featuring homemade pottery of all shapes and sizes, I pick out a small trinket bowl with a bright pink floral design on it for my mom. As we pass the jewelry store, a necklace in the window catches my eye.

"Hey, why don't you go to the bookstore, and I'll meet you there. I wanna look at something in here really quick."

"Okay." Tyler kisses me and walks off in the direction of the bookstore.

When I enter the store, I ask the salesperson if I can see the necklace in the window. It's a skeleton key on a long ball chain. She hands it to me, and I rub my thumb over the gothic details on the head of the key. Suddenly a flood of emotions fill my chest. Elation at the fact that I found a good man. Love for the man who says he's willing to be my boyfriend. Peace in knowing it's okay to finally give my heart to not just anyone, but to Tyler. This key is the sign I needed to know it was okay to move forward. I ask the women to gift wrap it for me and then I pay and run to catch up with Tyler.

When I find him in the bookstore, he has a copy of Oliver's new release in his hand and a woman is awkwardly hopping from foot to foot in front of him.

"Oh my gosh! It's you! I'm your biggest fan. I can't believe you're here. Would you mind signing my book for me?" she gushes when I join them.

Tyler looks at me and we smile at each other knowingly. "Of course I can. I'd be happy to. It's always nice to meet my biggest fan," Tyler says, returning his attention to the woman and taking the marker she's now offering. "What's your name?"

"Janine. J-A-N-I-N-E," she spells out.

"Janine, it's a pleasure. I hope you enjoy it." She squeals, and I wonder if I need to prepare for her to faint at his feet.

"Thank you, thank you, thank you," she cries while looking at the signature. "Can I take a picture?" she asks, still hopping.

"Sure can." She hands Tyler her phone and tucks into his side while he holds his arm out for a selfie. "There you go. Have a wonderful holiday, Janine." Tyler hands her back her phone.

She squeals again and scurries out the door to the shop. I can't stop laughing while Tyler pulls me in for a hug.

"That was so sweet of you."

"Let's just say that wasn't the first time it's happened." He smirks as we break apart.

"I bet. And I bet you and Oliver have some fun stories to tell."

"We do. But I'll never disappoint one of his fans. Come on, I want to check out one last place." Tyler takes my hand and pulls me out the door with him. We come to a stop in front of a hot chocolate stand beside the gazebo.

"We'll take two double chocolates with whipped cream," Tyler orders for both of us.

The jovial man behind the cart reminds me of Santa Claus and he chuckles with a *ho, ho, ho* as he hands us our cups. "Would you like some fresh cookies my wife made today?" he asks with a twinkle in his eye.

"Yes," I pipe up in excitement.

"Here you go." He hands us two large, warm sugar cookies sprinkled with red and green sugar.

"Thank you," I say, taking them from him while Tyler pays for our items.

"Thank you for stopping by. Don't forget to take a spin around the gazebo and make a Christmas wish. The magic is more powerful when the snow is falling," he offers with a wink.

I smile at Tyler and then follow him to a nearby bench to eat our cookies and drink the hot cocoa. The cookie's buttery goodness melts on my tongue and when I follow it with a sip of cocoa I hear sleigh bells ring.

"Did you hear that?"

"What?"

"Sleigh bells?"

"No," Tyler says with a curious look on his face.

We both look around and don't see anything. I start

to laugh.

"Why are you laughing?" Tyler asks.

"This place. Santa. Sugar cookies and hot cocoa. What have you done to me Tyler Hudson?"

"Me? We're here for your job. I didn't do anything, but you can't deny it is magical."

We both laugh, and I sit back and sip more cocoa waiting for the sleigh bells, but they don't come and I'm slightly disappointed. Maybe it's the cookie and cocoa combo. I take a bite and a sip and suddenly they ring out again. I laugh to myself and finish my treat.

"This will totally be worth the extra workout," Tyler moans.

"I'm happy that you don't take your diet too seriously to the point of obsession," I say.

"You haven't seen me during my cut phase. I don't plan on competing any time soon, so I'll wait until I've got you completely under my spell before I show you that side of me," he admits.

"It's that bad?"

"You know those Snickers commercials?"

"Oh."

"Yeah, but once the competition is over, it's game on, and pizza is the first thing I eat," he says with a laugh.

"Note to self. A well-fed Tyler is a happy Tyler."

"You got it. Are you ready to dance?"

I finish the last sip of my cocoa and we put our trash in the bin. As we ascend the steps of the gazebo "White Christmas" is playing through the speakers. I rest my head on Tyler's chest, and we sway to the music. I start dreaming of a white Christmas curled up with Tyler by the tree. Opening presents. He'd sneak in a small box. I'd open it and it would be the most beautiful engagement ring. He'd say romantic words. I'd say yes and jump into his arms. And then we'd be together for the rest of our lives. *Oh my gosh, who am I? Santa must have spiked my cocoa with Christmas magic!* In all honesty, I don't know if it's the cocoa, the magical setting, or the snow, but I don't want the fairy tale with Tyler to end. I let out a big sigh, and he squeezes me harder.

"Yeah, I'm pretty happy too," Tyler whispers in my ear.

"Thank you."

"For what?"

"For being you," I say.

"No trouble at all." He spins me out and brings me back in close to his body.

"What if I said I'm ready?" I ask.

"For what?"

"For all of this. You. Me. My job. Letting the world know I'm Tyler Hudson's girlfriend."

"Then I'd say I'm a very happy man."

"But what if—"

"Stop right there. Love is a risk, and it's one I'm willing to take with you," he says, holding my face between his hands. "Let me love you."

Without saying another word, I pull a box out of my coat pocket. "Here." I take his hand and place it in his palm.

"Isn't the guy supposed to give the girl the box?" he laughs.

"Just open it," I say, bouncing on the balls of my feet while I wring my gloved hands to calm my nerves.

Tyler opens it.

"I had no idea when I was going to give that to you, but after what you just said it seemed like the perfect time."

Tyler lifts the silver chain out of the box and notices a key attached to it. "Is this what I think it is?" he asks.

"Yes. I'm ready for you to have it. I will let you love me, Tyler. Don't make me regret giving you the key to my heart."

He lifts it and puts the chain over his head. "I'll never take this off. And I promise to always be kind to your heart." Tyler leans down and kisses me on the lips. When "It's the Most Wonderful Time of the Year" suddenly rings out of the speakers, it breaks our spell, and we pull apart. "Let's get back and warm up," Tyler says.

"I like the sound of that."

We link hands and run back to the cabin.

CHAPTER TWENTY-EIGHT
Tyler

WHEN WE GET back to the cabin, we shake off the snow and remove our outerwear and boots by the door.

"I think I'd like to get comfortable and put on my pajamas," Morgan announces as she shivers and runs her hands up and down her arms.

"I'll start a fire and then get changed too."

We kiss and part ways. She goes up the stairs and I grab some more logs and restart the fire. Once I've got it going, I join her upstairs to change. She's still in the bathroom when I'm done, so I grab the champagne I brought, rustle us up two glasses, and set everything on the coffee table and wait.

Morgan enters wearing pink fuzzy pajamas and oversized socks. She couldn't look more adorable if she tried. She's always dressed up, with her makeup just so, that it's nice to see her in a more natural look.

"You look comfy," I say, stretching out my hand to

guide her to my lap.

"Is that a nice way of saying I look terrible?" she asks, leaning back on me.

"No. Not at all. As a matter of fact, I like this natural Morgan."

"Thank you. What's all this?" she asks, motioning to the table.

"I brought champagne to celebrate your promotion. Now we have even more to celebrate." I pour the champagne and hand her a glass.

"To love!" I toast.

"To love," she repeats, and we clink glasses.

We each take a sip.

"What do you think?"

"It's good. Not too dry. One time a friend of mine splurged on the good stuff and I had to cut it with Sprite. I felt so bad." She laughs at the memory. "So apparently, you luck out because I have cheap taste."

"Are you calling me cheap?" I jest.

"Not at all. I meant in champagne."

"Oh, I'm glad we cleared that up," I continue to tease her. She laughs but quickly sobers.

"In all seriousness, I'm glad you could come with me today. It's been a special day, and I think I need to finally explain why I tend to keep myself closed off from most people."

"You don't have to."

"I'd like you to know." I nod for her to continue.

"When I was nine, my dad walked out on my mom and me. He came home from work and when my mom came out of the kitchen to greet him, he put his hand up to stop her. Said he was leaving. That he didn't love her anymore and walked back out the door. He didn't even take a bag. He just left. I watched my mom sink to her knees as the door closed, and the wail that she produced will haunt me forever. She stayed like that for hours. Just sobbing and staring at the back of the front door. I couldn't pull her away, so I finally brought her a blanket and pillow and she fell asleep on the floor that night. I tried my best to console her, but I was nine and trying to understand how he could leave me too." My eyes water and I pull her into me.

"I'm so sorry, Morgan. I can't imagine. I know what it's like to lose a father, but that hits differently."

"And now you know. I never wanted to relive that kind of pain."

"Thank you for telling me." I gently lift her chin so I can look her in the eyes when I say what I'm about to say. "I. Will. Never. Hurt. You like that. If something is wrong, we'll discuss things as a couple, and we will work through them. Thank you for giving me the key."

She nods with tears in her eyes. I gently sweep them away with my finger when they spill over.

"I never want to be the cause of these tears unless they are happy tears." She nods again and knocks me back on the couch with a hug.

"Thank you," she says, crossing her arms over my chest and looking down at me. "I knew there is something different about you Tyler Hudson."

I lean forward to give her a kiss on the lips. She starts to lean back so that I can sit upright, but we never stop kissing. When we stop to take a breath, Morgan removes my shirt. Then I quickly strip off her top and am greeted by two perky breasts ready to be devoured. I give them the attention they deserve, flicking her nipple with my tongue while kneading the other with my hand. Then I switch sides and she moans while pulling me down on top of her. She writhes below me. I'm rock-hard and ready, but I need to take my time. This time it isn't just sex.

I continue to suck and kiss down her body until I get to the sweet spot. Her body jerks in excitement as she holds my head in place while running her fingers through my hair. I stay where she wants me until she lets out a soft whimper of pleasure.

"I like that," she whispers, then holds out her arms for me to come back up. I quickly slide on a condom before positioning myself back on top of her. I pause and stare into her glistening eyes. The firelight dancing on her dewy cheeks. She's officially mine. She smiles as if she knows my inner thoughts and pulls me to her lips. Her mouth attacking mine. When we break apart, I whisper, "I love you."

CHAPTER TWENTY-NINE
Morgan

WHEN TYLER WHISPERS those words to me, my heart flutters because I feel it too. I finally know what all those people mean when they say, you'll just know when the right one comes along.

"I love you, too," I whisper back, pulling him flush with my body. The fire roars, and I want to roar beside it. I part my legs and welcome him in.

We've done this before, but this time it's different, and I'm ready to face whatever comes from doing so. My mind focuses as he tenderly enters me and connects us as one. I never understood how it could feel like your heart exploded and still be alive, but now I do. It's an all-consuming love that fills your entire chest.

"Yes!" I shout. Tyler stills.

"I haven't really done anything yet," Tyler whispers over my lips before huffing out a laugh.

"This. This moment right here. It's you and me. I feel it in every part of me."

"I do too." Tyler looks down to where we're connected then back up at me.

I raise my hips to meet his, giving him the go-ahead to proceed.

His slow pace creates a dizzying array of sparks inside me. When I can't take it anymore, I raise my hips again to urge him to go faster. He takes the hint and adjusts his rhythm with firm, powerful thrusts. The tension builds and before I know it, I'm enveloped in a white haze of silence as the world stops around us. There is no cabin. There is no fire. It's as if we're suspended in some euphoric plane that only we can ascend to together. Our groans of ecstasy as we come together bring me back to my senses, and I realize we're now heavily panting on the bearskin rug.

He gently lowers himself to my side and removes the condom. We pant in unison until our breathing is back to normal. The crackling fire flares from a gust of wind outside and we snuggle up under a blanket basking in the glow of this newfound love. Just as I'm drifting off to sleep, my cellphone rings in the distance. I'm not even sure where it is, nor do I care.

"Do you need to get that?" Tyler whispers.

"No. I don't care who it is. I never want to leave this spot," I say, curling into him.

"Neither do I. I really do love you, Morgan."

"I really do love you too, Tyler."

We pull the blanket tighter and fall asleep curled in one another's arms.

❄

"What the hell is going on here?"

I jolt awake to see Mr. Smyth, Tanya, Elliot, and Simon hovering above me. I pat myself down, making sure I'm covered, and look to my right where a tousled-haired Tyler is slowly waking with a grin on his face.

"Mr. Smyth. What are you doing here?" I ask, pushing wayward strands of my hair out of my face with one hand as I hold the blanket in place with the other as I sit up.

"I am here to make sure everything goes smoothly in my cabin!" he bellows.

A list of questions scroll through my head as I try to process the situation. What? His cabin? I thought this was Tanya's cabin. What time is it? How are they here already? Where's Alana? And …

"I see that you haven't abided by the rules of no sleeping with the models. Did you think you could just come up here for a weekend fling?" he barks.

"Mr. Smyth, if you could just give me a minute to explain everything," I say, holding out my arm as if it will somehow calm him down.

"I don't think there's anything to explain." He

stomps off in the direction of the kitchen.

"Nothing's going on between you two, huh?" Tanya says to Tyler.

"Tanya. Look. Let us get dressed and we'll explain everything," Tyler says, raising his arm but keeping his lap covered.

Elliot is fiddling with his collar. And Simon has an amused look on his face before walking out of the room.

"Elliot, let's leave them and go find my father," Tanya says, pulling on his arm. Elliot fans his face and winks at me as he follows her out of the room.

"Father? Did you know my boss was Tanya's father?" I ask Tyler as we stand while trying to keep covered.

"I had no idea. She's talked about him but never mentioned what he did. And I honestly had no idea her last name wasn't LeBoux," Tyler admits as we locate and pick up our discarded clothing together since we're sharing the blanket.

"I am in big trouble with a capital T, Ty. What am I going to do? I'm going to lose this job."

"I promised you it would be okay. I'll talk to them."

"No. Let me handle this. This is my account."

"If that's what you want," Tyler relents.

"Thank you. Let's get dressed." Tyler and I waddle up the stairs side by side and go to my room, where he drops me off and runs naked through the adjoining bathroom to his room.

I quickly dress in the clothes I came in since they're already out, but I do manage to slip on a new pair of underwear. I run into the bathroom, brush my hair and teeth, and slather on some tinted moisturizer. Tyler comes in and brushes his hair and teeth and then we walk back downstairs together. He tries to hold my hand, but I bat it away.

We find Mr. Smyth and Tanya talking at the kitchen table.

"Well, well, well. My star employee has fallen. Wow, I did not think you'd be this unprofessional, Ms. Pierce."

"Please allow me to explain," I say, folding my hands in front of me as if praying he'll understand.

"We have a company policy which you did not uphold and now I must terminate your employment."

"But sir—"

"No buts. I have arranged for your flight home. It leaves in three hours. My driver will take you to the airport. Then another car will be there to take you straight to the office where you are to clear out your things."

I hang my head in defeat.

"Mr. Smyth. May I say something?" Tyler asks.

"No, you may not."

"Dad."

"Tanya, I've made a lot of money in a very short time, and I didn't do it by cutting corners and making concessions. I don't want this to tarnish your name and reputation. I wanted to represent you and support you in a professional manner. This isn't professional. We'll get you a new model. I have several at my disposal that look like Mr. Hudson. We'll get them up here by this afternoon and we'll still be done by Sunday night. Monday tops."

"Dad, I appreciate that, but Tyler is a good friend of mine, and I'd like to finish the shoot with him."

"Fine. Get Simon and Elliot so we can get started."

"Ms. Pierce. I'll get the necessary files from Alana. You should go get your bags," Mr. Smyth says with a scowl.

"But—" Tyler and Tanya say in unison. Mr. Smyth holds up his hand to stop them.

"Your model is your choice. My employee is my choice."

I turn and let the tears fall as I walk to my room knowing they can't see my face. As I'm gathering my bags, Tyler comes in.

"I'm so sorry Morgan. I never thought they'd fire you. I thought I'd have a chance to explain."

"Don't. Just don't say anything else. I knew this was too good to be true. That I could have you and my job. I agreed to this, but I was foolish. Goodbye, Ty."

"Morgan, wait!"

"I have to go. It was the perfect night. Let's just leave

it at that so I can get out of this house with a little dignity left."

Tyler helps me take my bags to the car then kisses me on the forehead before helping me into the backseat.

"I'll call you when I get back, okay?"

"Don't."

"Morgan, don't push me away."

"Bye, Tyler." I give him a wave and get in the back of the waiting car.

He closes the door with a pained expression on his face. I can't look back as the driver pulls out of the driveway.

CHAPTER THIRTY
Tyler

WHEN I WALK back into the cabin, Tanya is setting up a makeup station on the dining room table.

"Where are Melanie and Victoria?" I ask, coming to stand next to her.

"I've been in so many makeup chairs I know what I'm doing. Since Dad wanted to come with me, I told him we didn't need the whole team," Tanya explains.

"Look. We need to talk. Your dad can't fire Morgan. It's not her fault."

"I've tried to talk him out of it, but he won't listen to me. I need you to get dressed first so I can put on your makeup," Tanya says while fiddling with a makeup brush.

"I'm not doing this until your dad agrees not to fire Morgan. We met right before she got her promotion. We're dating. This isn't some random model/employee hookup. We're in love."

Tanya's eyes go wide, and she drops the brush.

"What is that around your neck? I've never seen that before."

"The key to Morgan's heart. She gave it to me last night before she admitted she loved me."

"It's really love?" she asks.

"Yes. I love Morgan. We were trying to keep it a secret this whole time. And, speaking of secrets, when exactly were you going to tell me your dad owned the company?"

"Dad and I like to keep our personal business separate, so we don't tell anyone we're related, and I came up with the stage name. My dad was young when I was born and when my mom died, he got me into acting. He saw my potential. I honestly don't know how he built a company and ran me everywhere I needed to go, but he did. We didn't want to mess up all that we both built, so we've kept things separate, but we're really close."

"You know you could have told me. You know I keep my client list and what they tell me confidential."

"And you could have told me," she sasses back. "It's a choice my dad and I have made, and we've stuck to it. You can see he doesn't yield to change very easily."

"I see that."

"So, can you please get dressed so we can get this over with and you can get back to Morgan?"

"Is she still going to have a job?"

"I can't promise you anything, but I will ask my dad

to sit down with you and hear you out."

"Thank you." I nod. "Let's get this over with."

"Elliot! Bring in the clothes!" Tanya calls.

Elliot brings them in and hands me the first outfit. "A little flirting I could help you with. This I can't," he whispers.

"Tanya is going to try," I whisper back.

"Good." Elliot grabs his chest in relief and scurries off.

Once I'm dressed Tanya does my makeup and hair, where she makes a comment about not having to tousle it too much. I give her the stink eye and she leads me to the first position. We take shots by the fireplace, the bar, and the pool table. Then I change outfits three more times and take all the same shots. Mr. Smyth watches in the background with a stern look on his face. It's hard to read, but I must be doing something right because he hasn't barked any orders to the contrary.

Once we're done all the interior shots Tanya puts me in an all-black outfit to layer under the multi-colored puffer jackets I'll be wearing outside. Once Simon is ready, we trek outside, get the required shots, then we run in, warm up, change jackets, and do it all over again. By the time we're done I'm frozen and hungry. Thankfully, when we get back inside, the fire is roaring, and the dining table has been cleared to make room for a large array of foods.

"Please warm up and have a seat at the table when you're ready," Mr. Smyth says as we stomp the snow off our boots on the mat by the front door.

"Thank you. Could I have a word with you first?" I ask.

"You need to hear him out Dad," Tanya speaks up from behind me.

"All right then. Come into my office." He gestures for me to follow.

I quickly slip off my boots and do as he says. When we get to his office, he turns on the lights and sits behind the massive wooden desk. I take a seat in one of the chairs in front of it.

"Thank you for agreeing to hear me out," I start. He nods as he leans back in his chair and steeples his fingers together. "I wanted to let you know that Morgan and I are a real couple who are dating. We started before she got the promotion and tried to keep it a secret so she wouldn't get fired."

"I see," he says, giving me no emotional feedback.

"I think you should know, that while this should be none of your business because this deals with Morgan's personal life and not her work, I'm in love with her."

With my confession, his eyes go wide and then return to normal as he picks up the phone on his desk.

"Alana, I'm going to need you to go into the office for me today," Mr. Smyth starts. He explains why and when he puts the phone down, he looks at me. "Thank you for finishing the shoot for my daughter. I appreciate all you've done for her and your loyalty. She's spoken highly of you, and I'm happy to know my star employee will have a good man by her side. Now, I do believe you are in need of a flight home. Gather your things and my driver will take you to the airport."

"Thank you, sir." I hop up and run up the steps to my room, grab my bags, and run to the front door.

"Hey, weren't you going to say goodbye?" Tanya stops me.

"Bye Tanya. Thanks for helping with your dad. He's a good man. But now I have to go see my girl." I kiss her on the cheek as we hug then jump in the waiting car.

CHAPTER THIRTY-ONE
Morgan

I SPEND WAY too much on mini bottles of alcohol while flying coach home from the best-worst weekend of my life. I will be putting in an expense report before I pack up my things because that son-of-a-biscuit is going to pay for ruining my weekend. My tears of anger won't stop. I'm a blubbering mess, and the kind flight attendant sets a new bottle on my tray as she passes without asking.

I'll go and clean out my desk today, but I'll be going back to say my piece. I won't have anything to lose anyway. That man needs to know that I wasn't being unprofessional, and I do a darn good job, and he's a fool for firing me. I'm in love with Tyler Hudson! The man is mine, and just because his daughter is friends with him doesn't mean I have to give up my life for the company. And hello, daughter? Was anyone going to tell me that? I don't think I would have treated her any differently, but it would have been nice to know. So much for being in the loop.

Thankfully, the flight is short and I'm back on the ground before I'm completely sloshed. When I deplane, there is a driver holding a cardboard sign with my name on it. I walk up to him and let him know I won't need to pick up any baggage, and he escorts me to the car.

The Saturday traffic with tourists makes it take longer to get to the office building and it doesn't help the mood I'm in. I'm only thankful for the fact that the driver has water in a cooler back here and I can rehydrate after the flight.

When we pull up to the curb outside Smyth Advertising, I thank the driver, grab my bag, and then calmly walk into the building. I stride across the marble foyer, taking in the opulent features one last time before entering the elevator to get to my office on the second floor.

Alana is sitting at my desk and my steps falter. I expected to get in and out without anyone seeing me. A lump forms in my throat at the thought of my mentor being angry with me and having to tell her what happened.

"Alana?"

"Morgan!" She checks her watch. "Wow, that was a rough ride back. You should have been here an hour ago."

"You knew I was coming?" I ask incredulously.

"Jonathan called me and asked me to come in. I figured I'd work at your desk, so I knew when you got here," she says, motioning to her laptop.

"He told you what happened?" I ask. A blush of shame blooming on my face.

"He did." She nods.

"I'm sorry to have let you down. It's been an absolute pleasure working with you. I've learned a lot."

"Why don't you have a seat and let me speak." Alana extends her hand to the chair in front of my desk.

I leave my suitcase by the door and take a seat in the chair.

"Do you know why Jonathan asked me to be here?"

"To make sure I didn't steal anything on my way out?" I shrug.

"Not at all. He asked me to be here because he wanted me to tell you he made a mistake. He jumped to conclusions. After he let Tyler explain what happened he called me to tell me the whole story. He wanted to make sure that you did not clean out your office and that we did not lose you to another company." My jaw drops, and I quickly cover my mouth as she continues. "I understand that you and Mr. Hudson are dating and very much in love. That this was in no way a violation of our rules, and therefore, you are still an employee of Smyth Advertising, if you're still willing to be."

"Yes. Of course. I'd love to stay," I spit out.

"That's what I was hoping to hear. I'm sorry Jonathan didn't allow you to explain yourself, and we both promise to never do that again. We will make sure that you feel you can communicate with us and speak up when you need to. We sometimes get tunnel vision, and that's not fair to you."

"Thank you so much. I appreciate that. I think open communication is always good. I should have told you that first day when I saw that Tyler was going to be the model that we were dating, but honestly, it was all so new I didn't know what to say."

"It sounds like you're pretty sure now, huh?"

"Yes, I am."

"Good. It sounds like we all need to trust each other and communicate with each other," Alana admits.

"Yes, it does," I say, nodding my head still in slight bewilderment at the whole situation and the fact that Alana came in on a Saturday to make sure everything was straightened out.

"Now that we're in agreement, let's get out of here. Neither one of us needs to be working on the weekends. You need to learn a good work-life balance in the job so you don't burn out."

"Thank you. I will." I grab my suitcase and follow her to the elevator.

We hug as we part ways outside the building, and I walk as fast as my rolling case will allow back to my apartment. I've got to talk to Tyler.

CHAPTER THIRTY-TWO
Tyler

I CALLED ALLISON from the cab on the way home to see if she could get into Morgan's apartment to help me surprise her when she got home. Thankfully, I had access to the private jet and made it home in record time.

Allison greets me at Morgan's door when I knock.

"Hey there. I'm just about done," she says as I walk in, taking in the view.

Mini battery-powered tea lights are set up in various locations in Morgan's sitting area. The main lights have been dimmed and a bag from Martino's is sitting in the middle of her dining table with plates, silverware, and napkins set on either side of it. A bottle of wine is open, and the wine glasses reflect the flickering candles.

"This is perfect. How do you have so many candles?" I ask.

"You know what I do. I got a whole box from the company. They meant to send me one pack of twelve. I ended up with twelve packs of twelve. So let me know if you want some for your apartment!" I laugh.

"Where do you store all this stuff?"

"I have a closet. You don't want to see it," Allison admits dryly.

"Thank you so much for setting this up." I check my watch. "She should've been home already. I'm glad I made it before she got here."

"Hold on." Allison takes her phone out of her back pocket, taps on it, and then announces, "She's down the block. I better get out of here."

"How did you—"

"The app, remember?" she holds up her phone to show me and I see Morgan's moving dot.

"Oh, right. I'll have to download that app. I'll need to know where my girlfriend is when I'm not with her."

"Girlfriend?"

"I ... might have told her I love her last night," I sheepishly admit.

"Oh my gosh! That's huge." Her cheerful face breaks as she pauses. "Did she say it back?" she asks, squinching up her face.

"She did. And she gave me this," I say, holding out the key.

"Oh my gosh." She fans her face as tears form in her eyes. "Tyler that's such a big deal." She pulls me in for a hug and pats my back. "Okay, no time to get into this. She's almost here. I gotta go." She quickly backs away and pulls the door shut behind her. I laugh at Allison's whirlwind of emotions before taking off my coat and stashing it and my bag in Morgan's room. I make sure everything is just right then sit at the table and wait for her.

A few minutes later Morgan stumbles in the door and gasps at the sight. I stand and hold out my arms. She drops her bags and runs to me at full speed.

"I'm not fired!" she yells and squeezes me harder.

"I know. I was there when Tanya's dad called Alana."

"You were?" she asks, sliding down my body to stand on her own two feet.

"Yeah, I told him what happened and that we were in love. Then, without skipping a beat, he picked up the phone, called her, and told her to get to the office and stop you and to apologize to you for him."

"I was so mad the whole flight home. He wouldn't let me explain. He had all this faith in me that I'd do a good job in the position and then didn't trust me. It hurt more than getting fired."

"I can understand that," I say, rubbing her back.

"What made you do all this?

"You told me not to call you, so I came here instead."

"How did you have time?" she asks as I help her out of her coat.

"I got to take the private jet and called Allison to

help me out."

"Everything looks wonderful. And you got Martino's!" she cheers. "Thank you for doing all this for me." She leans in and gives me another hug.

"You're welcome. It's what you do for the people you love," I say, pulling out a chair for her.

"Just give me one more second to freshen up." Morgan runs to the bathroom and quickly returns. "All better."

She sits in front of a plate topped with fettuccini and meatballs. A carryout container of fresh bread sits between us, and I've poured white wine for us to drink.

"Thank you again for all of this. It's the perfect ending to a pretty emotional weekend," she says, raising her glass.

"Cheers to my new girlfriend," I toast.

"I like the sound of that. I haven't been anyone's in a long time. And I'm really happy to call you my boyfriend. I think I finally found someone worthy of the title."

"You most certainly have. I'm yours until you don't want me anymore," I admit soberly.

"That might be a long, long time."

"I can live with that."

"Let's eat. I'm starving," she says, lightening the mood, but I continue to watch her.

"I'm serious," I say, taking her hand and squeezing it.

"I know."

"Good. Because I didn't want you to have any doubts after giving me your key.

"I don't. Not anymore." She shakes her head.

When she takes a bite of fettuccini she lets out a soft moan.

"I think that's quickly becoming my favorite sound," I admit.

"Oh yeah? I kinda like that low growl you do when you do that one thing I like."

"If you keep talking like this, we might not finish our meal."

"Eating is overrated." She throws her napkin on the table.

I growl as I stand and hold out my hand. Morgan grabs it, and I pull her into the bedroom. We're out of our clothes in point two seconds, and I crawl over to her when she motions for me to join her on the bed. I worship her body until she screams out my name. I follow her screams with a few choice words on how much I adore her and then collapse on the bed next to her.

CHAPTER THIRTY-THREE
Morgan

I'M LYING PEACEFULLY in Tyler's arms when he speaks up, "You know, we should go on a real vacation. You have those travel brochures on that table by your door."

"Those are just for my dream board," I dismiss and curl into his side.

"What good is a dream board if you don't actually go on your dream vacation? Where would you like to go?"

Without skipping a beat I respond, "Somewhere warm," and wiggle in his arms.

"Hold that thought." Tyler slides his arm out from under me, jumps out of bed, and runs out of the room.

Naked running Tyler is as hot as you imagine it is. He returns with the brochures, tossing certain ones over his shoulder. When they land on the floor, I realize they all have snow in the pictures and laugh.

"All right. Pick one," he says, fanning them out in front of me.

I sit up and close my eyes, circling my hand over the

pile as if conjuring the perfect location, then pull one out and hand it to Tyler. I open my eyes and wait for his announcement.

"Drum roll, please."

"Brrrrrrr," I trill while clapping my hands on my thighs.

"We are going to ... Aruba!"

I jump out of bed and into his arms. He twirls me in a circle and then we fall back onto the bed.

"Are you really going to take me?"

"Of course I am," he assures me.

"I can't wait. I love you, Tyler."

"I love you too, Morgan."

We start kissing and after another round of well-executed pleasure, we get dressed and heat up the meals we left on the table. While we're eating, Tyler gets a phone call.

"It's Tanya." I sigh and gesture for him to answer it. He does and puts it on speakerphone. "Hi Tanya, I'm here with Morgan. You're on speakerphone."

"You guys worked it all out?"

"Yes, we did," I admit.

"I'm so happy for you guys." She claps then continues with the reason for her call. "So listen, I just feel awful about what happened, and I was thinking of making it up to both of you myself."

"You really don't have to," Tyler says.

"What if I told you it was an all-expenses paid trip to Aruba to celebrate my birthday?" she screams.

Tyler and I look at each other in disbelief. How could she know we just decided to go there? *Did her dad bug my apartment?* I look at the corners of my room for anything that might confirm that but have no idea what I'd even be looking for then turn my attention back to Tyler. "Guys? Are you still there?"

"We're here Tanya," Tyler assures her.

"Great. So you'll come?"

Tyler looks at me, and I look at him, and we both shrug.

"Tell us when and we'll be there," I say.

"I'll text you the details when I have them. Ta-ta for now," she coos before ending the call.

"We're going to Aruba!" Tyler and I cheer in unison.

"Next time, I'm picking somewhere in Europe," I quip, and we both laugh.

"Or a cruise," Tyler adds.

"Or both! A European cruise!"

"Cheers to that!" Tyler says, holding up his wine glass.

"Cheers to us!" I say, leaning in for a kiss before picking up my glass.

"Cheers to us," Tyler repeats.

We clink our glasses and laugh at our good fortune.

Made in the USA
Middletown, DE
14 October 2024